If Lucas hadn't been so astounded to see Lara, so perplexed at Josh Edwards calling her Caroline Kelly, he might not have allowed himself to be so easily shepherded back into the CEO's office. And the look on her face when she saw him. . . She'd looked frantic, ready to run—as well she might. . . He was dismayed to find that her eyes still had the power to tie his stomach in knots. She was different, yet the same. No earnest medical student now, but a sophisticated young woman with style. But a journalist? What the hell was she doing in journalism? She'd wanted to be a doctor. And her wanting it had. . .

Lara felt trapped, for his eyes said very plainly that he had not forgiven her.

Judith Worthy lives in an outer suburb of Melbourne, Australia, with her husband. When not writing she can usually be found bird-watching or gardening. She also likes to listen to music, and the radio, paints a little, likes to travel, and is concerned about conservation and animal cruelty. As well as romantic fiction, she also writes books for children.

Previous Titles

CONDITION CRITICAL
DOCTOR DARLING
LOCUM LOVER

DEADLINE LOVE

BY
JUDITH WORTHY

MILLS & BOON LIMITED
ETON HOUSE   18–24 PARADISE ROAD
RICHMOND   SURREY   TW9 1SR

*First published in Great Britain 1991
by Mills & Boon Limited*

© Judith Worthy 1991

*Australian copyright 1991
Philippine copyright 1991
This edition 1991*

ISBN 0 263 77454 6

*Set in 10 on 12 pt Linotron Baskerville
03-9111-52830
Typeset in Great Britain by Centracet, Cambridge
Made and printed in Great Britain*

CHAPTER ONE

'No! NOT under any circumstances!'

The deep male voice hit Dr Lara Montague's ears like a blast from a radio suddenly turned up loud as she paused to knock on the CEO's door. Her hand fell limply to her side and a chill shuddered through her. It couldn't be. . .no, it couldn't be him. . . Fate couldn't be that capricious. . . She must be mistaken. . .

She heard an incomprehensible but placatory-sounding murmur from South City General's chief executive officer, Josh Edwards, and then the other voice again, a tone milder but no less adamant.

'Medical students are different. They *need* to be there. This is a teaching hospital. But I will not have the Press gawking at life and death procedures and then writing it up as though it were some sensational television soap opera. Not when I'm operating.'

The strong dark tones wrapped Lara around with memories, bitter-sweet memories, that nailed her to the polished corridor floor when what she should have been doing was running. Why was Lucas *here*? The last she'd heard he was in America, doing so well that the likelihood of his return was so remote as to be impossible.

Josh Edwards must have risen and come closer to the door because Lara heard his next response.

'Caroline Kelly is a highly respected medical journalist, Lucas. I don't think. . .' Not knowing her by any other name, he had used Lara's pseudonym, which would mean nothing to Lucas, Lara realised with relief.

'No,' said Lucas Turnbull with finality. 'Women journalists are too squeamish in any case. We don't want people throwing up all over the place.'

Lara drew in a sharp breath of indignation.

Josh said with gratifying confidence, 'No problem there, Lucas. She's a doctor. If you'll just hang on for a few minutes you'll meet her.' He went on cajolingly, 'I'm sure you'll change your mind. She'll be here any minute.' He gave a slight laugh. 'She's a very punctual lady.'

Lara's toes curled in her black patent shoes. She hadn't always been, but Lucas Turnbull's passion for punctuality had left a lasting impression. And it wasn't the only thing he had taught her. . .

'I haven't got time,' Lucas said. 'Fix her up to see a few appendicectomies and cholecystectomies. . .'

'Run-of-the-mill stuff,' said Josh. 'It doesn't have the glamour or reader interest of heart transplants or even bypasses.'

'Glamour!' scoffed Lucas derisively. 'That's precisely what I mean. We're not here to titillate the tabloid voyeurs, Josh.'

Lara cringed a little at the familiar bluntness that had been sometimes so aggravating, but had been so much a part of the total honesty of the man. There had been times when she'd wanted to hit him—and now was one of them!

'If you hadn't been overseas until recently, Lucas,' replied the CEO patiently, 'you might have seen some of her material. She writes for *New Era*, one of our new Sunday broadsheets which is regarded as the best of the new crop of Sunday papers. Her editor's asked her to do an in-depth series for the colour supplement. Fairly clinical, but big on human interest. It's meant to be reassuring, not sensational. It's to coincide with National Heart Week.'

Lucas was still scathing. 'With photographs, of course. All in glorious, gory Kodachrome. No, Josh. It's no use your trying to persuade me. I had enough of media exposure in the States. I am not going to be pestered any more by chic little dolly-birds with tape-recorders and long-haired photographers looking for sensation. Not this early in the piece.'

The snarl in his voice made Lara wonder what had happened to make him feel so strongly. It must have been something bad. Something as bad as what she had done to him all those years ago. . .

God, I must get out of here! she thought, panic rousing her.

In a moment he was going to burst out of that door and see her. She didn't doubt that he would recognise her even though she looked rather different these days. Her once long brown hair was shorter now—it fringed her forehead to the edge of her naturally arched eyebrows, and was tucked sleekly back behind her ears, emphasising the high-cheekboned contours of her face. Long lashes shadowed her eyes, which were velvety brown and, as Lucas had once said teasingly, 'soulful as a spaniel's, sexy as a siren's'. She was tall, but she'd had to tilt her head to look Lucas in the eye at close quarters. He was over six feet.

The thought of coming face to face with him after all these years had a nightmare quality, and Lara shivered with a strange mixture of dread and longing. But she didn't really want to see him now. She'd do her series in another hospital. Frantic alternatives surged through her brain, but nothing would be as good as reporting on heart surgery at the South City General. Although it was renowned for other cardiovascular surgery, the hospital had only recently established a heart-transplant unit, the second in Melbourne. That was what the public wanted to hear about—and be reassured.

Lara unfroze and turned to make her getaway. She would phone Josh from the office, pretend a delay, and hear the bad news from him then. But she'd let the fascination of hearing Lucas's voice root her to the spot for too long. She was too late to avoid him. The door swung open and his large frame erupted from the CEO's office. As she involuntarily glanced over her shoulder she met his astounded gaze. There was no doubt he recognised her.

It was an eerie moment. Lara halted and stared, idiotically thinking what a beautifully fitting, no doubt horrendously expensive grey suit he was wearing and how well the soft grey shirt and maroon tie toned with it. Lucas had always dressed immaculately. Unconsciously she smoothed her hands down the double-breasted white jacket and bottle-green skirt she was wearing with a pale green blouse and high-heeled court shoes. Lucas had always liked smart clothes on a woman too. . .

Unaware of Lucas's astonishment and the consternation Lara was trying to hide, Dr Edwards said breezily, 'Oh, there you are, Caroline. I told Mr Turnbull you would be along any minute. He's a little bit doubtful about your project, but I'm sure if you explain to him. . .' He smiled broadly and stood aside to usher them both back into his office. 'If you'll just allow Ms Kelly to explain,' he said to Lucas in his best public-relations manner, 'I'm sure we can work out something that will be satisfactory.'

Good old Josh, Lara thought. He was the consummate diplomat, and proud of his ability to trouble-shoot in any situation, internal or external. He knew the value of good publicity and he knew how to manipulate his staff from the highest-ranking surgeon to the lowliest nursing aide. Anything that was good for South City General he would fight for with everything he had, and evidently he ranked her projected series on heart surgery as good for the hospital. Funds were always needed, and publicity generated funds. That was why he was taking a personal interest instead of leaving it to his PRO, who handled most Press enquiries. His personal attention was also a measure of his respect for Lara's professionalism. But Lara knew that Lucas Turnbull was not a man even Josh could manipulate.

'Kelly?' Lucas rapped, eyes piercing Lara with the sharpness of a needle. His gaze dropped to her left hand, expecting to see the evidence that explained her name change, and, not finding it, rose enquiringly to her face again.

Lucas's eyes were so dark that they were almost black. They could look, as now, devoid of expression, but Lara knew they could also show a range of emotion from tenderness to fury. His hair was still a smooth thick helmet of shining black, but there was a dusting of silver at the temples and a thread or two through the rest of it. It made him look even more distinguished, and at this moment formidable.

Lara's mouth was too dry for speech, but there was

no need for her to say anything. Josh said, 'Lucas, this is Caroline Kelly, the writer from *New Era*. Caroline, this is Mr Lucas Turnbull, a surgeon who has just recently returned from several years in America. He's the new director of the cardiac surgery department and the heart transplantation unit. Why don't we have some coffee and you can tell him all about the series you plan to write?' He grasped Lucas's arm and manoeuvred him back into the office, while throwing his other arm wide to invite Lara to join them. 'Come along in, Caroline.'

So that was why Lucas was able to throw his weight around, Lara thought. *He* was the new director. She'd been aware that someone had replaced Sir Lloyd Davies, the former director whom she had interviewed on his retirement, but Josh hadn't mentioned his name and it only now occurred to her that there had been no Press release yet, which was odd. Well, perhaps not, considering Lucas's apparent contempt for the media. As usual he would have got his way. If only she'd thought to ask, Josh would, of course, have told her his name.

If Lucas hadn't been so astounded to see Lara, so perplexed at Josh Edwards calling her Caroline Kelly, he might not have allowed himself to be so easily shepherded back into the CEO's office. And the look on her face when she saw him. . . She'd looked frantic, ready to run—as well she might. . . He looked at her as she sank into a chair, reluctantly, and crossed her legs. She was no happier about seeing him than he was about seeing her. He let his gaze drift over her slender, elegant figure. It was incredible running into her like this! He still felt he was having hallucinations.

But she was real. No doubt about it. She was slimmer

now, and even shapelier, and those prominent cheek-bones. . .the melting brown eyes—he was dismayed to find that they still had the power to tie his stomach in knots. She was different, yet the same. No earnest medical student now, but a sophisticated young woman with style. But a journalist? What the hell was she doing in journalism? She'd wanted to be a doctor. And her wanting it had. . .

'Sit down, Lucas,' a triumphantly smiling Josh Edwards was coaxing. He buzzed his secretary and ordered coffee.

Lara, feeling trapped, dug the nails of one hand into her palm under cover of the other resting in her lap. She wondered whether to admit that she and Lucas knew each other, and decided against it unless he did so. No doubt he would rather pretend they did not. His eyes said very plainly that he had not forgiven her.

'Well, now. . .' Josh sat behind his desk and regarded them expectantly. Then the phone cut him short. 'OK, I'll be right there!' he said crisply, and to his guests, 'Sorry, minor crisis, but I'll have to leave you to it. I don't know how long I'll be, but feel free to use my office for as long as you need it.' He beamed, obviously confident that they would come to an agreement. As he strode to the door the coffee arrived. 'Help yourselves,' he invited.

The door closed behind the CEO and the girl who had brought the coffee, making a hollow sound to Lara's ears. It was how she felt, left alone with Lucas: hollow inside. She glanced at him and found his dark eyes implacable, so she switched her gaze to the tray of coffee which was on the desk nearest to her chair.

'Shall I pour you a cup?'

'Thanks.'

Lara didn't even think to ask how he liked it. She lifted the silver pot and poured a full cup of black coffee and tonged one lump of sugar into it. Then she held it out across the gap between them. Lucas's broad long-fingered hand accepted it without touching hers. She noted the smoothly filed fingernails, the tiny tufts of hair between the finger joints—small details which almost choked her with unexpected poignancy.

'What a good memory you have,' he remarked drily.

Lara looked startled for a moment, then realised what he meant. 'Isn't it still black with one lump? Sorry, I should have asked. People do change. . .'

He stirred his coffee slowly. 'You have. The girl has gone and there's a woman in her place.'

She was irritated by the flush creeping into her cheeks. 'I'm still the same person,' she said rather archly.

'Why the name change? Married? Or married and divorced?'

'Not married or divorced,' she answered in clipped tones.

He did not comment, but inclined his head, considering her. 'Caroline? Why'd you choose that name?' He made it sound unsuitable.

'Caroline Kelly is my professional name. I just made it up. No Freudian significance I'm aware of! I'm still Lara Montague to my family and friends.' There was a tightness in her stomach as she spoke. She wasn't about to tell him why she used a pseudonym instead of her own name for her articles, why she preferred to let people who didn't know her think Caroline Kelly was her real name. It wasn't that Lara Montague was notorious exactly, just that there was less likelihood of anyone dragging up what she preferred to forget if she stuck to being Caroline Kelly, especially in medical circles.

'What happened to the big ambition to be a doctor?' His mouth tilted a little ironically.

Lara moistened her lips and, as her cup rattled on its saucer, wished her hand would stop trembling. 'I qualified. I practised for a couple of years. . .'

He raised one eyebrow slightly. 'And then? What on earth made you switch to journalism?' He sounded affronted at her defection.

She shrugged. 'I went overseas, met someone who asked me to write a few pieces for a medical journal, and somehow I got hooked.' She dredged up a smile. 'Funny how things work out sometimes.'

'You enjoy journalism?' There was outrage in his tone.

'I enjoy medical journalism.' She gave her words emphasis, but didn't add that she sometimes missed medicine of the hands-on type.

'Extraordinary.' Now he sounded like a medico confronted by a strange new medical condition.

He was eyeing her sceptically as though her explanation was as full of holes as a cellular blanket, which of course it was. Lucas had always been hard to fool, and she guessed he was busily trying to read between the lines now. But if he'd never heard the scandal about Dr Lara Montague he wasn't very likely to now. He'd been in America for several years when it had happened, and it hadn't been big enough news for the overseas Press or international medical journals.

Lara took a much-needed gulp of coffee and swallowed. Too much air went with the swallow and she spluttered uncontrollably. She clattered her cup on to the desk, slopping coffee in the saucer and over the polished surface. Coughing chokingly, she gripped her throat with one hand and the arm of the chair with the other as she fought for control.

Lucas was beside her in a second, 'Take it easy; don't panic. . .' His palm massaged her back firmly but gently and almost set off a worse paroxysm as, despite her present crisis, Lara's body involuntarily remembered the exquisite pleasure that Lucas's hands could engender. Oh, God, I mustn't ever think of that! she thought desperately.

'I'm—OK. . .' she spluttered.

'Don't try to talk. Just try to breathe normally.'

Lara tried, and finally succeeded. Sheepishly, between short bursts of coughing, she said, 'Sorry. It was hot and went down the wrong way. Damn, I seem to have spilled coffee all over myself and the desk.' Fumbling for a lace-edged handkerchief, she dabbed at the splashes on her white linen jacket and the arm of the chair. Lucas flipped a man-sized alternative out of his pocket and soaked up the puddles on the desk-top where her cup had slopped over. Lara objected. 'Don't. . .you'll stain it. . .'

He shrugged, picked up her cup and saucer and emptied the saucer into a pot-plant across the room, wiped it and set the cup back on it. 'Do you want to try drinking it the normal way?' He was standing over her as though she were a recalcitrant child being difficult about taking her medicine.

Lara felt a complete fool. 'Well, I suppose, if one's going to choke, a hospital is a good place to do it in.'

There was almost a smile on his lips, for the first time. 'It's given you a healthy colour!'

Lara clasped her hands over fiery cheeks. 'Do you mean I looked unhealthy before?' she demanded.

'You looked pale, but perhaps that was because you were taken aback to find me here.'

'I'll say I was.' Lara sipped her now cooling coffee gingerly. 'What *are* you doing here anyway? I thought the States had claimed you for good.'

Lucas did not sit down in his chair again but remained leaning against the edge of the desk, looking down at her. 'My father died a few months ago and it seemed a good time to return. My brother and sister are both married and living overseas and my mother is rather lonely, naturally.'

'They. . .your parents moved to Melbourne?' When she had known them the Turnbulls had been firmly entrenched in Sydney. His father had been an oil-company executive.

'Yes, several years ago. It was a career promotion.'

Lara stared for a moment at the long sensitive fingers clasping the coffee-cup and saucer as he drank. He was not wearing a ring either, but that didn't mean anything. Not all men wore a wedding-ring. She was consumed with a sudden desire to know whether he was married or not.

'Did you. . .bring a family back with you?' she asked.

'I'm not married.' His eyes were very black now, very intense as they pinioned her. He added, 'I've been too busy to get married.'

Lara placed her cup and saucer carefully back on the tray. 'So have I.'

He showed no surprise. 'Of course. You were always determined nothing would stand in the way of your career. I suppose journalism has its satisfactions and advancements too.' His tone was still edged with disdain. He didn't approve of her having abandoned medicine for a Press career. His disapprobation made her feel she had betrayed her calling for mercenary ends, and that made her angry with him. What did he know about it? What right had he to prick her conscience?

'Yes,' she answered curtly.

The silence that followed brought into sharp relief the unbridgeable gulf between them. The past loomed like a shadow on the sun, and Lara knew he would never change his mind, either about the medical articles she wanted to write or about her. If he hadn't already been adamant about not allowing the Press near his operating theatre he certainly would be now that he knew the journalist concerned was her. And she wasn't sure she would want to go through with it anyway, knowing that the man she would be most likely to see performing would be Lucas. It was significant, she thought, that he had not attempted to discuss the proposal. His mind was made up, and it would be an exercise in futility for her to try to change it. So she said nothing, but reached for her shoulder-bag, which she had placed on the floor beside the chair.

'I'd better be going,' she said. 'I'll talk to Josh later.' She rose, feeling awkward somehow, especially as he remained seated for a moment, languidly watching her, dark eyes scanning her with an X-ray vision. It was disconcerting to know that her anatomy was familiar to him, that he could easily visualise her curves, that he might remember the mole on her thigh he had once warned her to keep an eye on. That she could do the same with him brought a sudden flame to her cheeks and a warm fluid sensation deep inside that shocked her.

Lucas rose and stood looking at her, his mouth twisted ironically again, arms folded across his broad chest. He seemed about to say something, but Josh Edwards chose that moment to return.

'Ah, you're still here,' he said, sounding pleased. He looked hopefully from one to the other, his remark ending on a questioning inflexion.

'I was just going.' Lara glanced at her watch. 'I—I've got another appointment. . . I'll be in touch, Josh.'

The CEO sensed failure and looked at Lucas reproachfully. 'Well?'

Lara was almost at the door when Lucas said, 'We didn't get around to discussing Lara's series. . .'

'Lara?' Josh said blankly.

'My real name.' Lara paused to explain. 'Caroline Kelly is my pseudonym. Most people call me that so I hardly ever answer to my birth name these days.' She felt guilty, as though she were hiding something under the alias, but she had nothing to hide; nothing except damaged pride and some bitterness.

Understandably, Josh looked surprised that Lucas should have discovered her real name in so short a time.

Lucas provided the explanation Lara was reluctant to. 'We know each other from way back,' he said evenly. 'When Lara was a medical student we met at Sydney's Southern Cross Hospital. About ten years ago.'

Dr Edwards brightened. 'What a coincidence!' He clearly expected that this would have had a positive influence and was perplexed as to why it had not. 'I suppose you've been catching up on your activities since. But what about the articles Caroline wants to write, Lucas? Since you *know* her. . .' He beamed, confident that this would tip the scales.

Lucas's face gave nothing away, and Lara waited for his denial. She nearly fainted when Lucas calmly said, 'We didn't get around to it. Lara's going to have dinner with me tonight and we'll talk it over then.'

Lara's mouth fell open, and she shut it quickly. How like Lucas Turnbull that was! Always arrogantly assuming she would do what he wanted. She remembered the first time he had asked her out. It had been after a lecture he'd given to students. Because she had been so smitten by him she had failed to answer a question he'd fired at her, so he'd called her aside afterwards to lecture her further about her shortcomings in anatomy. Mortified, she'd vowed to spend every night studying the subject, and then he'd calmly said, 'Not tonight, though. You're coming out to dinner with me tonight.'

She should be saying no now, inventing a date, but just as on that long ago occasion she said nothing, just meekly accepted the *fait accompli*. Temporarily, she told herself firmly. She wasn't vindictive enough to call him a liar in front of Josh, even if he deserved it, but she wasn't going to have dinner with him. This wasn't like ten years ago when she'd been so surprised, so flattered, so utterly over the moon at being asked out by the dishiest—by popular opinion—surgeon ever to grace an operating theatre that refusal would have been unthinkable. She was no longer a susceptible medical student, and she certainly had no desire whatsoever to socialise with Lucas Turnbull. As she would shortly inform him. . .

Josh's smile broadened. 'What a splendid idea.' He winked at Lara. 'Good luck!' But she was already home and dry, his look said. Dinner with the director guaranteed it.

Tight-lipped, Lara glanced at Lucas, willing him to accompany her out of the office so she could tell him at once what she thought of his effrontery. If he didn't intend to allow her to observe operations, then why on earth was he pretending to Josh that he might be going to change his mind? And if he wasn't then why did he want to have dinner with her? A straight yes or no now was all that was needed. A disconcerting thought occurred to her: he wasn't thinking of dragging up the past, was he. . .?

'Thanks for the coffee, Josh,' Lara said.

Lucas held open the door and walked out with her. He accompanied her as far as the lifts. The corridor was empty and there was every opportunity for Lara to take him to task about his assumption that she would have dinner with him, but she couldn't seem to find the words. Lucas pressed the 'down' button and she knew she didn't have much time left.

'Lucas. . .' she began, but his intent look made the words she meant to say dry up on her tongue.

The lift was only a floor away and arrived promptly. As the doors opened, disgorging two passengers and leaving the lift empty, Lara still managed to miss her chance.

Lucas held the doors open for a moment as she entered. 'I'll pick you up about seven. What's your address?'

In spite of herself, Lara's resolve melted and she heard herself obediently telling him. As he released the doors and they closed she was left with a diminishing image of the man she had jilted, hand raised and complacently smiling.

'Damn!' she said to the array of lift buttons as she savagely punched the one for the ground floor. 'Damn him!'

CHAPTER TWO

AT ALMOST seven o'clock that evening Lara, in a satin
petticoat and bare-leg tights, looked at herself in the
mirror and pressed her lips tightly together. Was she
mad? Going out with Lucas Turnbull had to be madness.
He wasn't going to help her do her job—no way! All he
was likely to do was drag up old resentments and hurl
them at her. But surely he wasn't that bitter? It wasn't
as though she had jilted him for another man, and ten
years was long enough for hurt pride to heal. She didn't
blame him for being angry at the time, but on reflection
he surely must have *understood*. . .?

There was still time to say no. She could feign a
headache when he arrived. Lara reached for a lipstick
and applied it deftly. She realised she wasn't going to
stand him up, admitted that she was curious about him,
and denied that a curious ache deep inside her was
anything to do with the fact that she'd loved him once.
Thought she had loved him. If she truly had then she
would have married him, wouldn't she? She wouldn't
have got cold feet.

Lara raked her fingers roughly through her hair,
tilting her head and stretching her neck to ease the
tension that was growing with every minute. Reliving
old arguments was pointless. And if Lucas had asked
her out just so he could be saracastic about her journalism and make barbed remarks about fickle females then

she was crazy to put herself in the position of letting him
do it.

She set her mouth determinedly for a few seconds,
tugging at her now wild hair. In spite of herself, her
resolve evaporated.

'Face it, Lara,' she muttered, 'you want to go. Just
this once.'

The compulsion she felt made her angry, but she
stopped fighting it and pulled on a sleek purple woollen
dress with a dropped waistline and wrist-length sleeves.
She clasped a jade necklace around her slender neck and
a matching bracelet over her right wrist and slid her
watch back on her left.

She studied her ringless fingers for a moment with a
wry little smile. Dirk was anxious to put a diamond on
her left hand, and perhaps it was time she stopped
holding back. Dirk Hoekstra's job as a *New Era* photographer gave them plenty in common. Why was she so
reluctant to commit herself? She was nearly thirty, and
most of her contemporaries were married with families,
even those with careers. She wanted to get married and
have a family, but she was leaving it a bit late.

Lara shook herself angrily. She was coming close to
having regrets, which was dangerous. And it would
never do for Lucas to suspect it. As she fastened the
straps on her black high-heeled sandals she wondered
idly about his love-life. She was surprised he wasn't
married, but she didn't doubt there'd been plenty of
women in his life. Lucas had always been a man who
enjoyed female company, and Lara doubted if he was
any less passionate now than he had been a decade ago.
Maybe he was glad she'd jilted him; maybe he preferred
to be unattached and playing the field. Maybe. . .

With a sudden shudder of apprehension Lara straightened up and ran a comb through her hair. The glossy waves fell elegantly in a skilfully cut style that needed no elaborate attention.

'If he thinks. . .' she muttered, shoving cosmetics into a black-beaded bag.

The doorbell rang, a long ring, then two short bursts. Lara caught her breath. Lucas's ring. Her heart began to flutter as she fumbled in a drawer for a handkerchief. She took a last look at herself, grabbed the black-braided purple jacket that matched the dress and hurried into the hall. It annoyed her that she felt flustered. It usually took an earthquake to ruffle the calm which had stood her in good stead as a doctor and as a journalist.

She dropped her bag on the hall table. The clock in the living-room was chiming seven. On the dot! she thought and took a deep breath as Lucas rang the doorbell again.

As she opened the door he was looking at his watch. He switched his gaze to her and she caught a flicker of relief skidding across his eyes.

'I thought you might have stood me up,' he said bluntly.

She could hardly blame him for suspecting that of a girl who had jilted him. 'Why would I do that?' Lara opened her eyes wide and smiled. To cover her nerves she rattled on, 'Are you coming in? I can offer you a sherry or whisky. . .?'

'Thanks. We've got time,' he said, and marched in, looking around with interest as he followed her into the living-room. 'Nice flat.'

'I like it.' Lara faced him, daring no more than a glance at his face. 'Well, what'll it be?'

'Whisky, thanks.' He paused to examine a painting on her wall.

'Soda or water?'

'Water.'

Lara poured the whisky and a small sherry for herself. 'Sit down,' she invited. 'Make yourself comfortable for a few minutes.'

He lowered himself into an armchair and she placed his drink on the lamp table beside it. She perched on the arm of the sofa. 'Cheers!'

He lifted his glass, and regarded her thoughtfully. 'Cheers!'

This is going to be awful, Lara thought dismally. It's going to be the most agonising evening of my life. What on earth are we going to say to each other?

'I spent an hour at the state library this afternoon,' Lucas said. 'I looked up a few of your articles.'

Lara dropped her eyelids. 'Oh, really?' She waited nervously for his comments.

'Very good,' he said. 'Your medical training shines through.'

She flared suddenly. 'You don't have to be patronising!'

'Still defensive, I see,' he murmured with infuriating calm.

'Not at all. I was shortlisted for an award for medical journalism last year,' she told him with justifiable pride.

'I know. And you should have won it. It was a very thorough and well-researched series you did on Sudden Infant Death Syndrome. Emotional, but not over the top.'

Lara laughed modestly. 'You have been busy! You

found out all that about me in one afternoon. Why did
you bother?'

He shrugged. 'Curiosity, I suppose.'

She came back sharply, 'Is that why we're having
dinner? Curiosity?'

'I dare say you're as curious about me,' he suggested
languidly, 'as I am about you.'

'Mildly,' she conceded, 'but, in view of——'

'In view of the fact that you jilted me some ten years
ago, you feel a little bit awkward, is that it?' The dark
eyes were searing.

Lara's cheeks burned. 'I was going to say, in view of
the fact that you have already refused to let me observe
cardiac operations, there seems little point.' She gripped
the stem of her sherry glass tightly and her voice rose.
'For God's sake, Lucas, you're not taking me out for the
pleasure of harping on what happened ten years ago, are
you? Surely that's all dead and buried now? I thought
your invitation was just a friendly gesture—for old times'
sake. But if you've got some twisted idea of giving me a
hell of an evening in revenge for my reprehensible—yes,
I admit it, it was a lousy way to treat you—behaviour
ten years ago, then you're not the kind of person I
always thought you were. Surely, in retrospect, you must
have *understood*?' The times, she thought, she'd said that
to herself to quieten the guilt that at first had constantly
nagged her! She hadn't wanted to hurt him, or humiliate
him. Out of breath, she fell silent, annoyed that she had
let him rile her.

His face was impassive as though he was unmoved by
her sudden tirade. After looking at her steadily for a
moment, he said very quietly, 'Yes, Lara, I understood.
That was the hard part.'

Lara felt tears at the back of her eyes. It was cruel having to remember. Oh, why did he have to come back and dredge it all up again?

'I think it might be better if I didn't have dinner with you,' she said.

He rose and put his empty glass on the buffet. 'Nonsense. We've cleared the air, haven't we? We've mentioned the unmentionable. Let's go and eat and behave like the civilised adults we are.' For a moment his expression was almost apologetic. 'We've both had something of a shock, I guess, meeting so unexpectedly. It was bound to rattle a few skeletons!' He smiled encouragingly, the kind of smile that bowled over small children and little old ladies, and. . . Lara Montague.

The air was not cleared, but Lara was disarmed. 'Well, it's a pity to be all dressed up and going nowhere, I suppose.'

She ran her gaze over his tall immaculately clothed frame. He was wearing a dark blue suit tonight, a crisp white shirt and a grey patterned tie. His hair was sleeked back and the silver gleamed at the temples. There were lines around his eyes that she didn't remember because they wouldn't have been there ten years ago, and the creases in his cheeks had deepened. But he was still the handsomest man she'd ever known, and one glance from those hypnotic black eyes still had the power to tie her stomach in knots. How different would the past decade have been, she suddenly wondered, if she'd really loved him and they'd married. . .?

Lara was not surprised to find Lucas driving an upmarket car. The sleek grey BMW parked outside her block of flats gleamed in the light from the street-lamp, and the deep upholstery sighed luxuriously as she sank into the passenger-seat.

'You know Melbourne?' she asked as he swung the car away from the kerb.

'I spent a few holidays here in my teens and when I was at med school. It never appealed to me then—too cold and wet, and the beaches weren't up to much. How about you?'

'I've got used to it. I was never a great beach-lover. I freckle!'

He chuckled. 'Yes, I know!' He glanced at her, even more amused because he had succeeded in making her blush. 'There's a red gene in you, Lara. It shows when the light catches your hair, and when you lose your temper.'

Lara bit her lip, won over. 'If I shouted back there I'm sorry.'

'We won't mention it again,' he said. 'We're letting bygones be bygones, remember?'

'I'm willing.'

Lara concentrated on the changing traffic-lights at the intersection they had just smoothly approached, and noted that they were heading towards the city. She wondered where Lucas was taking her. He hadn't said. That was typical. It had been a kind of ritual, surprising her. As though she were a child to be given treats, Lara thought now, which of course she had been back then. Nineteen and thinking herself so adult, so sophisticated; yet in some ways she had been so immature.

'Do you think you'll stay in Melbourne now?' she asked as the lights changed and they crossed the intersection.

'My mother would like that. And, since I've been

lucky enough to fall into a job that suits me, I dare say I will.' He slid a smile in her direction. 'I'm no surfie these days!'

'It's raining,' Lara said as a fine mist deposited droplets on the windscreen.

'That's Melbourne for you!'

The smooth hum of the windscreen wipers filled the silence for several blocks. Lara couldn't think of anything else to say. She felt nostalgic and sentimental all at once, thinking of warm summer days in Sydney, lying on secluded beaches, eating out at the newest restaurants, perpetually astonished that Lucas was dating her, and then overwhelmed when he asked her to marry him, and then. . . She tried hard to shut a mental door on her defection, but the chinks kept letting the chill memories through.

It was raining steadily when they reached the Charcoal Cat, which was the kind of restaurant that had a doorman with an umbrella to usher customers from their cars across the footpath. Watching from the restaurant porch, Lara was relieved to see Lucas find a parking spot only few yards along the street. The doorman strode after him and sheltered his return.

'I haven't been here before,' Lara whispered as they entered.

Lucas smiled at her. 'I brought my mother here for her birthday. Her first outing since the funeral. It was very good.'

And very expensive, Lara deduced, gazing at the gilt and velvet décor, glad she'd worn her best outfit.

'How is she taking it, really?' Lara murmured as they sat down.

'Hard. She and Dad were a perfect match.'

'It's sad. She must be very lonely now. It's fortunate that you could come back to be with her.'

'You must come and say hello some time,' Lucas invited, as the waiter placed menus in front of them.

Lara was startled at the suggestion. 'Lucas, I don't think. . .' Mrs Turnbull had been furious with her, had refused to speak to her after she'd called off the wedding. It would be terribly embarrassing for them to meet now. And surely Lucas would not want to see her again himself after tonight?

Lucas frowned. 'My mother doesn't bear grudges, Lara. When I told her who Caroline Kelly was she was very excited. She admires your articles. She said she'd love to see you again.'

'Yes—well, maybe some time. . .' Lara said, filled with dread at the prospect, despite what he'd told her.

To Lara's relief, the wine waiter hovered, taking Lucas's attention from the subject, and he did not return to it. The wine and meal ordered, Lara asked Lucas about his years in America.

'It was a marvellous experience,' he admitted. 'The quality of equipment, medical staff and nursing staff was the very best where I was working for most of the time. It was a great hospital; very innovative.'

'And hot on public relations?' Lara guessed drily.

His mouth twisted into irony. 'And how! It was sometimes like running a side-show.'

'Is that why you're so against someone like me observing?'

He gave her a fixed look. 'Right!' His mouth firmed into opposition. 'It can get so that people forget there are life-and-death battles going on under the arc lights. There's always a risk of losing concentration when you know you're under scrutiny, even when they're only in a viewing-room. It's not good medicine. It's hazardous.'

'Have you ever lost concentration? I can't believe you would. . .'

'Everyone is fallible,' he said shortly, and, although his eyes were shuttered, Lara was sure that a faint twitch at the corner of his mouth betrayed an emotion he was trying not to show. Lara felt intuitively that his strong feelings were the result of some deeply personal trauma, not just the annoyance of having the Press around. She wanted to ask, but the private pain she sensed in him deterred her.

'What do you think of the SCG's cardiac surgery department?' she asked.

'First rate,' he acknowledged. 'They've already notched up some remarkable achievements. I'm only sorry to have missed working with Sir Lloyd Davies. His shoes will be hard to fill.'

'I interviewed him about setting up the heart transplantation unit just before he retired,' Lara said. 'I'll never forget those piercing blue eyes.'

Lucas laughed. 'Nor, I dare say, will a long line of petrified medical students, interns and nurses. He has a formidable reputation. Was he difficult to interview?'

'He was charming. Tough, but once he discovered I was a doctor he stopped trying to put me down. Like you, he didn't approve of my change of career, though.'

Lucas did not retract his own disapproval. 'You were so dedicated, Lara, that I find it hard to believe you'd change just on a whim. Just writing a few pieces for a medical journal hardly seems an adequate reason.'

They were getting on to dangerous ground. Lara chose her words carefully. 'Sometimes you fall into doing things you hadn't really intended doing. I don't regret it.'

'What were you doing before you went overseas? Where did you do your internship?'

'At the Southern Cross. Then the opportunity came up to join a team at the Lovell Institute doing research on MS, so I went there for a year.' There, it was said. Now all she had to do was keep her answers to his questions circumspect. And change the subject as soon as she could.

He was unsurprised. 'Because of your mother?' His voice was low, sympathetic.

'Yes.' Her mother had contracted multiple sclerosis and had died when Lara was twelve. Lucas knew of her deep feelings about that loss.

'But you didn't stay with it?'

The ground was shakier now and Lara tried to hurry the conversation past the danger zone. The one thing she did not want to talk too much about was that disastrous year at the Lovell Institute. 'I wasn't really cut out for research.' To him it must sound like another example of her fickleness.

'It can be frustrating.' Lucas was watching her intently, making her nervous. 'What were you doing?'

'I was mainly involved with work on trying to isolate the cells in the immune system which attack the body's nervous system.'

'Why did you quit?'

Lara avoided looking directly at him. She couldn't tell him the truth. 'I was restless. I wasn't sure whether I wanted to continue doing research or go back to the wards. I like people. . .'

'So you decided to interview them instead of cure

them? Was it a case of cold feet perhaps? Did you give up medicine because you're squeamish after all?'

Lara flinched at the 'cold feet' gibe. 'It wasn't quite like that. As I said before, I fell into journalism by accident rather than design.' That made her sound more fickle than ever, Lara thought, and she was sure Lucas thought so too. His mouth was hard, his eyes penetrating. She was a woman who didn't know what she wanted, who still kept changing her mind, he was doubtless thinking. She didn't wait for him to press her further, but changed the subject.

'Sir Lloyd Davies rarely operated in his last couple of years,' Lara said. 'He was mainly an organisational head. How do you see the position, Lucas?'

He laughed softly. 'You sound just like a real interviewer!'

'I was just asking,' Lara answered edgily.

'And I shall answer you,' he said, reaching across the table to give her hand a reassuring squeeze to show he wasn't really mocking her. 'I'm a surgeon, Lara, and I don't intend to let organisation overwhelm me. I'll be in Theatre as often as I can.'

So he didn't intend to be some lofty figurehead, Lara approved. It didn't surprise her. Lucas had never had much patience with administration. He had always been more concerned about saving lives. With him in control, there were bound to be some changes of emphasis.

He went on emphatically, 'And until I've settled in I don't intend to waste my time on accommodating the Press.' His mouth was a firm line. 'And even then my co-operation will be seldom and reluctant.'

Lara warned, 'Dr Edwards won't like that. He thinks the SCG should maintain a high profile in the Press.'

Lucas remained implacable. He gave a slight lift of his shoulders, a determined smile. 'I think I can handle Josh.'

Lara could not help a laugh. 'I'm sure you can.' She shook her head reminiscently. 'You haven't changed, Lucas. Nobody pushes you around, do they?'

His eyes glittered for a moment. 'Except you,' he murmured, and Lara flinched.

The emotional charge between them was, however, mercifully defused by the arrival of their meal. Lara concentrated on the food and wine while she searched for a safer topic of conversation. That wasn't difficult if she stuck to medical matters.

'I've been reading up on coronary atherectomy,' she commented. 'What's your opinion, Lucas? Is it really as good as it's reputed to be? Is the procedure going to reduce the need for surgery significantly?'

Lucas teased softly, 'Is this on or off the record?'

She relaxed as they moved away from the personal area. 'Off. I'm not going to get out my notebook or tape-recorder on a night off.'

'Nevertheless, we shouldn't be talking shop,' Lucas said, lifting his glass of wine to his lips. 'But the answer to your question is yes, it looks very promising for some bypass situations. I was involved in clinical trials in the States and I think we're going to see it used increasingly.'

'Because it's not as invasive as bypass surgery?'

'Open-heart surgery should always be the last resort. You can perform an atherectomy under local anaesthesia and it only takes one to two hours. The revolving blade slices off the build-up of plaque in the arteries and no vein grafting is needed.'

Lara nodded. 'You insert the catheter with the athero-cath attached via the groin as for an angiogram?'

'Precisely.' He smiled indulgently, and said, 'Now, let's give medicine a miss. Seen any good plays lately? Films? Ballet? Read any good books?'

Lara laughed. 'You want recommendations?'

Their eyes locked. 'You know my tastes,' he said.

Lara lowered her gaze, unsettled by his. 'There's a wonderful play at the Playhouse,' she told him, 'which I'm sure your mother would love. That's why you asked, isn't it?'

He nodded. 'I must try to persuade her to go out occasionally. She's brooding too much.'

Lara said, 'Don't force her. She needs to grieve. She'll resume her life when she's ready.'

He gave her a sharp look.

Lara went on, 'It's only natural to be anxious, but it'll make it harder for her if she feels she has to do what you want, go at your pace. Don't make her feel she's being a nuisance and a worry.'

He looked more surprised than offended by her gratuitous advice. 'You mean she might think I've got over Dad's death too quickly?'

'You should both try to appreciate that people handle things differently,' Lara said.

'I miss him too,' Lucas said simply. 'I regret now that I was away these last years and saw so little of him.' A regretful smile crossed his lips. 'We waste so much time, Lara, not realising how valuable it is.'

He forked a mouthful of food to his lips, but before he could dispose of it his pager shrieked an urgent summons.

'Blast!' He reached into his jacket pocket and silenced

it, already half out of the chair. 'I'd better get to a phone.'

He was back in seconds, a deep frown between his eyes, his whole body emanating urgency. 'Got to go, I'm afraid. This is a big one. And one of my surgeons went off sick with flu this afternoon.'

'It's all right,' Lara said. 'I'll get a cab home.' Her sense of disappointment was keen. She looked up into his face, certain it was for the last time. She might run into him casually somewhere, but he wouldn't ask her out again. His curiosity had been satisfied. It was ridiculous wanting it to be otherwise. He didn't want to resurrect the past and, if she had any sense, neither did she.

Lucas looked hard at her for a moment, then grabbed her arm. 'If you want to write that series you'd better come along and get started on it. There's a good chance you'll see a triple or quadruple bypass tonight.'

'But you said——' Lara was nonplussed.

He was impatient. 'I know. I changed my mind. Now, are you coming or are you going to stay here and finish your dinner?'

Lara leapt up. 'I'm coming with you, of course.' A surge of elation filled her. She didn't know why he'd changed his mind, but that didn't matter. The amazing fact was that he had agreed, and she wasn't going to miss the opportunity. Tomorrow he might change his mind again.

She grabbed her jacket off the back of the chair, and Lucas signed the hastily prepared bill. In seconds they were running through the darkness and rain to the car, the doorman having now vanished from his post.

Lucas did not make conversation. His face was set

rigidly as he negotiated the twists and turns between the restaurant and the hospital to get there in the quickest possible time. Lara did nothing to distract his attention. She felt tense with apprehension in case he suddenly regretted his invitation, and with a sense of anticipation that was only partly journalistic. It was, she realised, the imminent medical experience that was causing such a surge of adrenalin to make her whole body tingle. And the fact that she would be watching Lucas operate for the first time in ten years.

CHAPTER THREE

THE theatre Lucas was using had a viewing-room with a large window which afforded a good view of the area of action. It was empty when Lara entered. She had not dared to ask if she could observe inside the theatre. This was victory enough.

It was ten-thirty p.m. She drew out her notebook, glad that she always carried it with her. She wrote the time on the blank page, then began to make notes on the scene in the theatre. Although she was outside, there was a certain intimacy with what was going on only a few feet away. Lara felt strange, like being a student again. Of course, then she had often observed from close to the operating table, and had done her stint assisting. Influenced by Lucas, she had once wanted to go on and become a surgeon, but she had taken up the research job instead. It was a pity, she thought, that she hadn't chosen surgery.

There was a great deal of activity in the theatre, but no sense of panic despite the fact that they were dealing with an emergency. Nurses were quickly but calmly laying up the instrument tables and connecting and testing equipment. Lara's pen flew across the notebook page, converting what her eye saw—what her eye hardly needed to see, since the procedures were familiar—into phrases that later she would knit together to make it interesting to the newspaper readers, with just the right amount of clinical detail, just the right amount of emotion and drama. Her gaze flicked over the instruments, the neat array of forceps, haemostats, scalpels, retractors, scissors and other vital implements, and noted the complex anaesthetic equipment and heart-lung machine, and all the other pieces of high technology that cluttered a modern operating-room.

There was no sign of Lucas. He had left her almost as soon as they arrived at the hospital, taking time only to call a nurse to look after her.

'Dr Montague will be observing,' he'd rapped out briskly. 'Show her where to go and give her a cup of coffee.' He'd glanced at Lara with a faint smile. 'Looks as if I'll have to wait a while for mine!'

She'd voiced her thanks, but he was already rushing off. Still astonished at his change of heart, Lara had followed the young nurse, determined to be as unobtrusive and as little trouble as possible. Her high heels, however, had clicked loudly on the polished vinyl floor in contrast to the nurse's soft-soled shoes, making her feel conspicuous.

Jenny, the nurse, knew only a few sketchy details about the emergency, but eagerly aired her knowledge. Lara asked questions, but did not reveal that she was a journalist—the well-known Caroline Kelly.

'The patient is someone pretty important,' the nurse told Lara. 'A judge, I think. He was giving a speech at a dinner when he collapsed. I heard Dr Vernon say he didn't fancy his chances much.'

'Who's Dr Vernon?'

'Cardiologist.'

'Still, it's amazing what skilled surgery can do,' Lara remarked conversationally as they paused for her to collect a polystyrene cup of black liquid which was probably as tasteless as that from most coffee dispensers.

That the patient was newsworthy was a bonus, even though his collapse would doubtless be headlined in the daily Press tomorrow, while her article would not appear for some weeks yet. By then, though, she'd know if the operation had been a success or not. If he pulled through maybe he'd agree to talk to her. . .she could do a great background piece if he'd let her use his name. . .

'Mr Turnbull's fantastic,' confided the nurse with admiring wide eyes. 'I flat with a theatre nurse who's scrubbed for him a few times, and she says he can do a triple bypass faster and more efficiently than anyone. She says he told them he doesn't like patients to be kept open for a second longer than necessary.'

'Does he operate often?' Lara asked.

'Oh, yes. He's the hands-on kind of director. He doesn't just let everyone else do the real work. He's very popular with the med students and interns too. They all think he's great. . .' she giggled '. . .especially the girls! He's so good-looking!'

Lara was wryly amused. 'Yes, I can imagine that.' Lucas had always had a good deal of charisma. Look at the way he'd swept her off her feet when she was a medical student!

Now, alone and staring at the as yet empty operating table, Lara waited for the fantastic Mr Turnbull to arrive. A green-capped and gowned figure entered the operating-room and began to check equipment—the anaesthetist. Lara bent her head to scribble some more notes, and when she looked up the patient was being wheeled in, and seconds later Lucas appeared.

It was sometimes hard to recognise people when they

were gowned and capped, but Lucas's tall broad frame
and air of authority were unmistakable. Lara was sure
that he had completely forgotten her by now, so she
drew in a sharp breath when he suddenly glanced in her
direction and lifted one hand slightly in silent acknowledgement. She lifted hers in a brief response, but he was
already directing his attention to the patient.

Lara craned forward, anxious to catch every move in
the sterile environment beyond the glass. Lucas was
giving instructions. And suddenly Lara was aware that
she could hear his voice! There was a sound system in
the booth which had been turned on for her benefit. She
could hear every word, every rustle of gowns and chink
of instruments. It was almost like being out there. . .

'. . .almost like being there,' she wrote in a lightning
scrawl across her notebook page. 'Ten-thirty-five, and
you can feel the tension, although everyone looks calm.
And now they're moving in, like runners at their starting
blocks, waiting for the starter's gun. . . The surgeon
looks briefly around the semi-circle of intent pairs of
eyes. . .hard to tell male from female. Scrub nurse is a
man, I think. . .you can tell instinctively from the way
he moves. . .and now the surgeon says calmly, as though
they're just leaving for a picnic, "Let's go, shall we?". . .'

Lara paused, pen against her lips, as Lucas made the
first incision. She gritted her teeth at the sound of the
patient's sternum being split and scribbled furiously,
anxious to capture the immediacy of it all, knowing that
her own experience could fill in later the clinical details
she might miss now. What was important was the
atmosphere, the drama, and the reassurance that a first-
hand observer could convey. Her personal impressions

right here and now were important for the realism of her
finished article.

'The lights are strong and the surgeons are sweating.
The scrub nurse leans over and wipes the sweat from
Lucas's brow, but he hardly seems to notice. They're a
good team, working in perfect unison. . .few words. . .
Pity the patient can't see the skills, the care, the smooth
teamwork. . .'

Lara glanced at her watch every so often and jotted
down the time. 'Time passes quickly,' she wrote. 'Mr
Turnbull believes a patient should not be kept open
longer than absolutely necessary—ask him about
that. . .'

She leaned her chin on one hand and craned her neck
to see what was happening, but there were too many
people in the way. Lucas turned his head and muttered
something inaudible to the anaesthetist, who made an
adjustment to the supply of gas and analgesic. Halothane
and pethidine, Lara guessed, making another note to
query that. As she looked up again Lucas was frowning.
Was he worried about something? Was this going to be
one time his skill would be in vain? There were drops of
perspiration collecting on his forehead again. Why
doesn't the scrub nurse notice and wipe it? Lara thought
crossly.

For a moment everything became terribly still as
though the group around the patient had been turned to
stone. Then a surprised female voice said, 'He's gone!'

There was an infinitesimal moment of shock before
the tableau melted into action, mainly at the anaesthetist's end of the operating table. Green gowns obscured
Lara's view for a time. She thought there was probably
a problem with the endotracheal tube. Lara craned

forward, tense and waiting for what seemed like an eternity.

Then she heard a muffled, 'That's it,' from the anaesthetist, and the relaxation in the rest of the team was almost palpable. Whatever the crisis, it had now passed and the operation was proceeding. The judge was not dead.

At midnight Jenny came in with more coffee and sandwiches.

'I thought you might be hungry,' she said.

Lara thanked her.

'How's it going?' Jenny asked, glancing at the scene.

Lara shrugged. 'OK, I guess.'

'He's lucky,' said Jenny confidently. 'Mr Turnbull's the best!'

Lara smiled. 'You sound like a nurse with a big crush on a surgeon!'

Jenny pulled a face. 'Some hopes! Men like Mr Turnbull don't look twice at girls like me. Not when there are top lookers like Teresa Ioannidis around.'

'And who is Teresa Ioannidis?' Lara enquired with an unexpected pang that almost felt like, but surely couldn't be, jealousy.

'She's a theatre nurse. She's there now. The smallest one. She's mad about him, so the gossips say. Somebody saw them out together once, and I heard they were caught smooching in the lift, so I suppose there must be something in it. Lucky Teresa! Still, it's not surprising. You can't tell with her cap and mask on, but she's a real head-turner—dark hair and huge eyes and smooth olive skin. She's Greek. She's got a gorgeous figure too,' Jenny finished enviously, adding, 'I'd better go. See you!'

Lara sipped her coffee and nibbled the sandwiches.

She found herself staring at Teresa Ioannidis and for some reason resenting the closeness of the theatre nurse to Lucas, the obvious rapport there was between them which she might have thought merely professional if Jenny hadn't gossiped. But she shouldn't be surprised. She knew Lucas must have women friends. It was nothing to her any more. She had relinquished her claim on him long ago, and he wanted none on her now.

Lara's eyes began to feel heavy despite the coffee and food. Once she almost dropped off and her pen skewed across the page as her head sagged momentarily. She got up and stretched, massaging her aching neck, then went for a walk down the corridor and into the Ladies, where she splashed cold water on her face. It was two a.m. Not much longer now, she thought.

Another coffee perhaps would help to keep her awake right through. She found the surgeons' coffee-room, which was deserted, but to her delight there was a percolator bubbling. She helped herself to a cup of decent aromatic coffee and sat down in one of the comfortable armchairs. The coffee was too hot to drink at once so she placed it on the table near by. One or two people drifted in and out, but no one asked who she was and why she was there. She leaned back in the chair and, without meaning to, fell asleep.

A babble of voices roused her some time later, and she started up guiltily to see Lucas still gowned, but minus cap and gloves now, looking down at her. The lines of strain and weariness were deeply etched in his face, but there was a glint in his eye that told her the answer to her question before she asked it.

'How's the patient?'

'As well as can be expected,' he answered cautiously.

Then he said with a hint of mockery, 'How long have you been here? Missed the main feature, did you?'

Lara glanced at the time. 'Only the last half-hour. I came in for a coffee and. . .well, I must have dropped off.'

'Coffee's cold now,' said Lucas, glancing distastefully at it.

'Can I get you one. . .?' Lara extricated herself from the chair.

He shook his head. 'Not now. I'd best take you home. . .'

'Lucas, I can get a cab,' she protested.

'I'm going home myself,' he said, 'so I may as well take you. It's on the way.'

'Lucas. . .' The slightly breathless voice belonged to a small dark-haired nurse also still gowned, who rushed over to him. She stopped when she saw Lara. 'Oh. . .hello. You're the journalist?'

Lara guessed who she was before Lucas's introduction. 'This is Lara Montague, Teresa,' he said. 'Lara, Teresa Ioannidis.'

Teresa eyed Lara warily.

Lucas prompted wearily, 'Did you want me for something?'

The way she looked at him told Lara that she most certainly did, but it wouldn't be what she was going to say publicly.

She drew him a pace away. 'I'm sorry to bother you now, but it's about next Sunday,' she said anxiously. 'I'd like to let Mother and Dad know. . .'

Lucas raked his fingers through his hair. 'Of course. Yes, well, barring emergencies, no problem.'

Teresa beamed at him. 'Great!' she said on a little

sigh of relief. She glanced back at Lara. 'I hope it was interesting for you,' she said affably, but her eyes were penetrating and suspicious. 'We'll be seeing you quite often, I gather.'

'From time to time, I hope,' Lara answered, without looking at Lucas. 'Until I've completed my series.'

Lucas said abruptly, 'I'll be back in a few minutes, Lara. Get your things and wait for me in the foyer.'

He walked off, Teresa in tow. She was tugging at the ties on his gown as they went through the door. For some reason that small service, which nurses did for doctors all the time, looked very intimate. There was no doubt that, for Sister Ioannidis, Lucas was her very special surgeon. And she was obviously anxious for him to meet her parents. That knowledge gave Lara a very peculiar pang.

'I hear you're going to be writing us up for *New Era*,' said a warm-toned voice at her elbow, making Lara jump. 'I thought Caroline Kelly must be a doctor. Congratulations on your articles. They're excellent.'

Lara felt a glow of pleasure at the compliment, if a little dismayed that her secret was now revealed. 'Thank you,' she said, turning round to smile at the man who had come up to her. He was thirtyish, and had a friendly smile and candid blue eyes.

'You were the anaesthetist,' she said, sure she recognised him.

'That's right. Graham Butterworth.'

Lara extended her hand, which was grasped in a firm handshake. She was also not unaware of a glint of masculine approval in his eyes. Maybe she didn't look such a wreck at this hour as she supposed! She was, however, more eager for information than flattery.

'There was a respiratory problem about halfway through the op, wasn't there?' she queried.

He groaned. 'I'll say. The endotracheal tube. God, it always happens at a crucial moment, but it was only a temporary hiatus. The patient wasn't really in any danger, although for a moment it looked like it.'

He took a swallow from the coffee-cup in his hand. 'Can I get you a coffee?'

Lara cast a glance at the cold coffee she had left on the table. 'Thanks, but I don't think I'll bother now. I expect Lucas will be back in a minute. . .he's offered me a lift home.'

Graham gave her a speculative look but did not comment on that. 'Come and meet a few other medicos while you're waiting,' he generously offered. 'It'll help to smooth your path on future occasions. Some of us don't care for publicity, but the powers-that-be are hot for it. I suppose Josh talked Lucas into letting you observe.'

'I don't think so. He was adamantly against the idea at first, but he changed his mind later.'

Graham leaned close and whispered in her ear, 'When he discovered what gorgeous legs you've got?' Before Lara could frame a crisp retort he was saying, 'Ah, there's Lou Vernon. Cardiologist,' he added.

Lara could hardly believe her luck. She felt intrusive, being dragged to meet people who must have been very tired after a long night's work, but she was received politely, if a little warily, especially by Dr Vernon. There had apparently been a number of other casualties requiring emergency surgery of various kinds that night, and for a few minutes a number of people passed in and out of the coffee-room. Lucas was away a long time, but the interim passed quickly for Lara.

She and Graham Butterworth were still deep in conversation with one of the young registrars, who had flippantly suggested that, any time she wanted to see *him* perform, she could scrub up and lend a hand, when Lucas returned for her.

'You'll have to put your notebook through the auto-clave, though!' Graham was saying with a laugh.

'Ready, Lara?' Lucas was frowning as though he disapproved of her fraternising with his colleagues.

'Yes, of course. . .'

'Come on, then.'

He muttered a brusque goodbye to Graham and the other doctor, and strode off. Lara lingered only long enough to voice her thanks to Dr Butterworth and then hurried after him. He was halfway along the corridor leading to the lifts when she caught up with him.

'You must be dead on your feet,' she said. 'It was a long op.'

He shrugged. 'There are longer ones. We had a bit of a respiratory problem, that was the trouble.'

'Yes, Graham Butterworth was telling me. . .'

He looked down at her. 'Didn't take you long to get to know everyone.'

Lara ignored the trace of sarcasm. 'I had a fair bit of time to fill in.'

He held the lift doors open for her. 'Sorry I kept you waiting. You would have been quicker by cab.'

'It didn't matter at all. Graham saw I was alone and came up for a chat. He thought it might be helpful to me if he introduced me to a couple of people. I was grateful.'

Lucas gave a short laugh. 'Graham likes the Press. Especially if they're female and good-looking.'

They went down in silence. Knowing how weary he must be, Lara did not try to make further conversation, even though there were dozens of questions she wanted to ask. Lucas's adrenalin was probably still running, the way it usually did even when a crisis was over, but Lara decided to keep her quizzing until another time. She was still astounded that he had changed his mind about allowing her to watch him operate and she didn't want to do anything to jeopardise the situation. She was also curiously buoyed up because she *would* be seeing him again after all.

Dawn was breaking as they left the hospital, and by the time they reached her suburb, the sky was lightening rapidly. Cloud-cover in the east was pink-tinged and rapidly turning gold as the sun rose. The streets were practically deserted.

Lucas finally said, 'Sorry about your ruined dinner last night. I guess you must be starving.'

'Not really. . . A nice young nurse brought me some sandwiches and coffee at midnight.'

'Lucky you! Well, I could do with some breakfast. Let's find a café that's open. Do you know of any that serve breakfasts?'

'Not around here,' Lara said. She glanced at him hesitantly, then took the plunge. 'If you want to come up to my place I'll make you some breakfast. You can put your feet up there.'

She thought for a moment that he was going to refuse, but he was just concentrating on cornering a sharp bend. 'OK,' he said as they slid to a halt at traffic-lights. 'If you're sure you don't mind. You must be ready for bed.' He glanced at her. 'You can take the day off?'

She nodded. 'I more or less work my own hours. I'm on assignments, which is a bit like being freelance except that I'm salaried.'

'Sounds very secure.'

'Nothing is secure in journalism,' she replied.

'Still, with two strings to your bow, you'd have no trouble flitting from one profession to the other, I dare say,' Lucas remarked as they sped across the intersection.

Lara did not reply.

At her flat he did not relax in the living-room as she suggested, but followed her to the kitchen and watched her make porridge and toast. He had shaken his head admonishingly when she'd suggested bacon and eggs. 'I'm trying to look after *my* arteries!'

They ate at the kitchen table, and Lucas actually suggested that Lara ask him anything she wanted to about the operation. She took the opportunity gladly, but felt she was wearying him too much, so she suggested he have a second cup of coffee in the living-room and catch the news on television.

'I expect your judge will get a mention,' she said.

Lucas collapsed at one end of the couch and, after switching on the television, Lara sat at the other. There was indeed a news item about the judge who had collapsed and been rushed to hospital for emergency bypass surgery. His condition after a quadruple bypass was stable, the newsreader said cheerily. Lara glanced at Lucas for his confirmation of the accuracy of the statement, and saw that he was fast asleep. For a moment she felt an almost overwhelming tenderness, a desire to smooth from his face the creases that even sleep had not erased and, crazily, a desire to kiss the slightly parted, relaxed mouth. She pulled herself up abruptly. Nostalgia was one thing, but there was no need to indulge it that far!

He looked uncomfortable, though, head slightly askew on the back of the couch. She hesitated for a moment, not wanting to wake him, then went into her bedroom for a pillow and placed it against the arm of the couch, with a cushion beneath for extra support. Gently, she eased off his slip-on shoes and raised his legs on to the couch. This caused his upper half to slide down until his head touched the pillow and he was lying full-length. He protested only briefly at the change of position and did not wake fully.

'Just making you comfortable,' Lara said softly, and covered him with the tartan rug from the end of her bed.

She stood looking down at him for a moment. It was the last thing she had expected—Lucas Turnbull sleeping peacefully in her flat. A wave of longing suddenly swept over her, a need to feel his arms fold around her, his lips touch hers. . .

'Oh, God, no!' she breathed silently. 'Don't let me *want* him. Not now, not after all these years. Don't let me wish I hadn't jilted him. . .'

She turned quickly away. She couldn't wake him and turn him out now. She clasped her head in her hands, then, desperate for distraction from the sleeping man on her couch, took her notebook out of her bag, and, taking a clipboard with sheets of A4 attached off her desk, she curled up in an armchair and proceeded to write the first draft of her article. She was not tired now; her doze at the hospital seemed to have revived her, and she worked steadily for half an hour. But her second wind soon faded and, leaning her head back to gaze at the ceiling for inspiration, she closed her eyes and immediately drifted off.

When she awoke she was dismayed to find it was nearly midday. Lucas was still apparently dead to the world. She rose quietly and crossed to the couch. A lock of black hair swept across his forehead, and she noticed for the first time how enviably long and luxurious were the dark lashes that lay on his cheeks. His breathing was steady and his body was sprawled in an attitude of total relaxation. A dark stubble across the lower half of his face gave him a faintly dangerous look.

Leave him, Lara thought. He moved slightly without wakening, and the lock of hair slipped lower. Without thinking, Lara reached out and lifted it off his face. As she did so his eyes flicked open, looked dazed, then puzzled.

'Sorry. . .' she muttered, embarrassed and drawing back quickly.

An odd expression came into his eyes and his hand reached up and clasped her wrist tightly. 'What's the time, Lara?'

'Midday.' She felt a tremor run through her as his fingers held her fast, and she could feel her pulse beating under them. He did not let go.

He gave a resigned chortle. 'Sorry I flaked out on you. It's been a heavy week.'

'No problem. I've been asleep too. Luckily the phone hasn't rung and no one's paged you. I hope that means all's well with the judge.'

He nodded. 'I'd better get in there and check.' He was still holding her wrist and didn't want to let go. It was ten years since he'd touched her skin, and just clasping his fingers around her wrist reminded him of how smooth and satiny she was. Almost involuntarily he drew her down, amused at the surprise in her eyes, gratified at the lack of resistance.

He gave her a sudden jerk, which threw her off balance to sprawl on top of him.

'Lucas. . .what are you doing?' With her chin almost on his chest, Lara found herself rather too close for comfort to the dark eyes that mocked her.

He didn't give her time to regain her composure. The rising flush in her cheeks, the absence of anger in her low tone encouraged him, and he wrapped his arms around her, pulling her close enough to be kissed.

Which he proceeded to do with a thoroughness that left Lara breathless, skin tingling from head to toe, and even more disturbing sensations uncoiling deep inside her. The feel of his warm, hard body under hers, his persuasive lips manipulating hers so seductively, was so familiar that she could almost believe she had missed it all these years.

Lucas dragged his mouth from hers, cupped her face in his hands and smiled. 'You haven't changed, Lara. You're still as beautiful, still as sexy———'

'And you're an opportunist!' she said.

'We were good together,' he murmured, stroking her jawline with his thumbs.

Lara wrenched her head from his restraint and scrambled up to sit on the edge of the couch. 'Yes—*were*, Lucas. Past tense.'

He grasped her hand and toyed with her fingers, taking them to his lips and nibbling the tips. 'What's wrong with the present?' His other hand stole lightly

along her thigh, and his reach was long enough for him
to flatten a palm across her stomach and then trace the
softly swelling outline of her breast. Its passage over her
nipple, despite the covering of clothing, was a white-hot
reminder of why Lucas had managed to change her
strong views about sex before marriage when she was
nineteen. He was pulling her back on to him again,
sliding his hand warmly under the neckline of her dress
and beneath the fine cotton of her bra.

'There's something rather exotic about making love at
midday,' he murmured against her ear, dragging the
blanket which had covered him from between their
bodies and flinging it on the floor. 'Something deliciously
hedonistic. . .' He moved sensuously against her rigid
body, and clasped his hands hard across her buttocks,
pressing her into his pelvis, as he kissed her again, more
slowly and persuasively this time, waiting for her
response and then matching his to it as he slowly took
her on an increasingly desirable journey. Even the
roughness of his unshaven skin was tantalisingly erotic.

Well, why not? Lara's brain said treacherously. He
was right—they had been good together. Marvellous!
Fantastic! And it hadn't been easy to throw it all
away. . . What was wrong with a little lovemaking now?
It had been a long time. She hadn't spent the interim
having affairs. Somehow there had never been anyone
she'd wanted to go beyond a few kisses with. She didn't
imagine it had been like that with Lucas, though.

He had just discovered that the buttons on the bodice
of her dress concealed snap fasteners and that, once
undone, the top pushed easily off her shoulders. Lying
the way she was, her full rounded breasts hung forward

tantalisingly, and he had no trouble releasing them from the flimsy bra and petticoat.

'Ah. . . Lara. . .so lovely. . .' he murmured huskily, bringing his mouth to each rosy tip with a sigh of pleasure.

To have him in her bed again, Lara was thinking dazedly as desire swept through her like wildfire, would be so wonderful. But, even as she let herself indulge this tempting fantasy, a vivid picture entered her mind. Like a douche of cold water she saw Teresa Ioannidis smiling up into Lucas's face, proprietorially helping him ungown, and, regarding her, Lara, with suspicion. They were lovers, she was sure. A girl as lovely as Teresa, with her sensuous dark beauty and her obvious willingness, was hardly likely to find resistance in a man like Lucas. She had been arranging for him to meet her parents, what was more. Maybe Lucas was even halfway serious about the girl.

Lara, mortified at how far she had allowed him to take advantage of her weakness, drew back, crossing her arms across her chest. 'No, Lucas,' she said in a small ragged voice. 'I don't want to. . .'

She had aroused him to an almost unbearable pitch. 'Lara. . .what do you mean. . .*why not*?' He couldn't believe that she could suddenly deny her feelings, which he was sure had been as fierce as his only a moment ago.

She scrambled off the couch, and he was too stunned to try and stop her. 'I don't think we should make love, that's all,' she said, dragging the dress back across her shoulders. 'I—I don't think we should complicate things.'

'But, Lara. . .' Her eyes were scared, yet desire still softened them. He held out his arms to her and saw that it was difficult for her to deny him. But she had a phenomenal strength of will. She always had. And paradoxically he admired her for it. Sadly, he let his arms fall. She wasn't going to let herself get involved with him again. Graham maybe, or any other man, but not him.

'Don't let's talk about it,' she pleaded. 'We're both a bit het up.' Finding it difficult to face the disappointment and frustration in his eyes, she moved away. 'Would you like to have a shower? I could make you some lunch before you go. . .'

He swung himself off the couch. 'Yeah, I wouldn't mind. It'd save going home.' He grinned suddenly, good humour returning. 'And it's more comfortable here than the facilities at the hospital.'

'Go ahead, then,' Lara invited, relieved that he had accepted her refusal in good grace. 'I'll get you a towel.'

She ran to the linen cupboard and extracted a large fluffy bath-towel, which she threw to him as she showed him through her bedroom to the *en suite* bathroom. 'Take your time,' she said. She glanced over his somewhat dishevelled appearance. 'You'll have to make do with the shirt, but I can run the iron over your suit while you're showering.'

He grinned. 'I'd better be free with your deodorant, I guess!'

'Help yourself. In the cabinet. You'll find some disposable razors there too.' She took his jacket as he peeled it off, but as he started undoing his belt she said, 'You can leave your strides over the chair. I'll come back for them.'

Followed by his mocking laugh at her modesty, Lara went out. When she heard the shower going she crept back and retrieved his trousers. His shirt she put on a hanger to air. It smelled faintly of his own tangy deodorant, with a whiff of iodine overlaying it, but it wasn't offensive. He could wear it again, she thought, smiling as she remembered how fastidious he had always been, liking clean shirts every day, sometimes twice a day. He'd always kept a couple at her place before, but he'd have to go without today.

She plugged in the iron and pressed his suit. She was still ironing the creases in his trousers when he appeared in his under-shorts, bare-chested, barefoot and so potently masculine that it took her breath away. He had shaved, and looked less like a gangster on the run now but no less dangerous, she thought in an agony of longing. The sooner he got dressed and out of here, the better. Teresa or no Teresa, she only had so much will-power.

'I ought to take you out to lunch,' he said, 'seeing I messed up your dinner last night.'

'I'm not complaining.' Lara placed the iron back on the stand. 'Here you are. Did you have a tie?'

'Wasn't it in my jacket pocket? No? Well, I expect I left it at the hospital. Not to worry. I've got nothing on today that requires me to be a picture of sartorial elegance! We won't go anywhere flashy for lunch.'

'Lucas—I've got to go to the office,' Lara invented. 'I'd rather just have a quick sandwich here. I need to shower and change too. . .and I know you're anxious to get back to the SCG to check on your patient.' His closed look made her relent a little and add, 'Some other time maybe?'

He came over to the ironing-board to take the trousers from her. 'Are you angry because I tried to seduce you?'

'No.' Disarmed by real or feigned contrition, she smiled. 'Flattered, actually!'

'You slapped my face the first time I tried,' he recalled. 'Quite a little wildcat you were, so indignant. . .'

Brown eyes flashed, but not without humour. 'I didn't want you to think I was easy.'

'And now? Is it the same now?'

He leaned over the ironing-board and tilted her chin, forcing her to look at him.

Lara stepped back, out of reach. 'No. I just don't want to start anything, that's all.' She was glad the ironing-board formed a barrier between them.

'There are. . .other men?' The thought of it aggravated him.

'None of your business,' she rebuked lightly, 'and I don't want to know about your other women, thanks.'

'Lara. . .' His voice was plaintive.

'Now what?' Despite the ironing-board, his closeness, his near nakedness, was setting her nerves jangling.

'Are you still afraid of being committed? Because this time I wouldn't ask for commitment. . .'

Shocked by the bluntness of his proposition, Lara ran her tongue swiftly over dry lips. 'Lucas, I don't want to have an affair with you. If that's what you need there must be plenty of women dying to oblige, I'm sure, so let's just forget this morning's little lapse, shall we? Let's both just carry on with our lives as though our paths had not crossed again. I'm very grateful to you for letting me observe in your theatres, and I hope you won't change your mind because——'

'For heaven's sake, I'm not vengeful!' He looked

steadily at her for a moment, then turned and went back to the bedroom to dress.

Lara put the ironing-board away and made a pile of sandwiches and a pot of tea. Lucas had always liked tea with lunch. Earl Grey tea. She was glad she had some. She was not so glad now that she had embarked on the new series. In spite of what she'd said to him, she had half hoped that Lucas might change his mind. She couldn't renege herself because it would be too difficult to explain to the others involved. So she was going to have to see quite a lot of him during the next few weeks whether she liked it or not, and the prospect gave her a strange kind of painful pleasure.

CHAPTER FOUR

'WHERE the hell have you been?'

Grant Jermyn, deputy editor of *New Era*, greeted Lara's appearance in his office the next afternoon in his usual abrasive manner. At the same time he tossed a pale green pill into his mouth and poured a glass of mineral water to swallow it.

Lara frowned. She was not intimidated by him now— although she had been at first—because she had soon discovered that Grant's bark was far worse than his bite, and that its ferocity varied according to the state of his ulcer.

His ulcer was playing up today, she decided. But surely that wasn't her fault?

'I've been writing up my first article for the new series on heart surgery,' she said, and dropped the disk on which it was now written in front of him.

He held it tentatively. 'You didn't have any trouble at the hospital?'

'It was touch and go,' she answered, dropping into a chair uninvited. You could stand for a week and collapse before Grant would think to offer you a seat. 'But by a coincidence I happen to know the new director of the SCG cardiac surgery department from way back.'

Grant smiled salaciously. 'Oh yes—a few favours. . .'

Lara felt her colour rising. 'Definitely not!' She did not take offence, however. Grant was, like many newspapermen, a cynic.

He massaged his diaphragm gingerly, and Lara said, 'You give that ulcer of yours a rough time, Grant. You ought to ease up a bit. Learn to relax more.'

He scowled. 'What do you want me to do? Transcendental meditation?' He gave a roar of laughter, then winced.

'It wouldn't do you any harm, and probably a lot of good,' Lara said seriously. 'You'll be in real trouble one of these days if that ulcer perforates. Then you'll be rushed off for a gastrectomy.' She knew his ulcer was a stomach lesion rather than duodenal. Like many people on first meeting a doctor, he'd given her a run-down of his physical fitness, or lack of it, then ridiculed her when she'd been naïve enough to offer advice, and had kept her for fifteen minutes listening to his low opinion of the medical profession.

'Trouble with you quacks,' he said now, 'you can't wait to cut people up. Pack of butchers. Well, nobody's going to plunge the knife into my guts.'

'They'd have a job,' agreed Lara, straight-faced, and he scowled at her again.

'Well, what's the score? What else are you going to get? When are they going to do another transplant? That's what we want.'

'I don't know,' Lara answered. 'I have to play it by ear. I'm hoping for a transplant, of course, but heart transplants don't happen every day of the week, Grant. They'll call me when there's something on that's newsworthy. I want to get the right mix of stories. There's plenty of time before National Heart Week.'

He twisted the disk in his hand. 'Yeah. I guess so. Now, what about photographs? We need pictures.'

'That might be tricky,' said Lara, who had not yet

broached the subject with Lucas. 'I doubt if we'll get any in Theatre during actual ops. Lucas Turnbull—he's the director—is not keen on publicity or any kind of distraction.' Seeing incipient apoplexy in her boss's face, she rushed on defensively, 'There are problems. An operating theatre has to be absolutely sterile. . .'

'I know that. You can gown a photographer and sterilise his camera, can't you? It's been done before. They take record shots themselves, don't they?'

Lara ignored the interruption. 'Whoever does it may have to take shots from the viewing-room, or else a mock-up after an operation if I can get everyone to co-operate.' She added, 'Failing that, we could probably borrow some of their record shots——'

'That's not what we pay our layabout photographers for!' he complained, going red in the face.

Lara flinched on behalf of Dirk, who was certainly no layabout and had taken many a prize-winning photograph.

'I want some pics with drama, not straight record shots,' Grant insisted. 'You need professional talent for that.'

Lara smiled as he redeemed himself with the last comment.

'I'm afraid Lucas is not going to be very co-operative,' she said.

Her boss looked ready to blow a fuse. 'I'd better get on to Josh Edwards. This Turnbull fellow can't be a law unto himself.'

Lara smiled knowingly. 'Oh, yes, he can! I'll fix something, don't worry,' she said hastily, fearing for Grant's ulcer.

He nodded. In a little over a year he'd become used

to trusting this tall, elegant young woman with the flashing brown eyes and sexy legs to deliver the goods, and so far she hadn't let him down. It was her medical training that made her reliable, he supposed, paradoxically ignoring his customary derogation of the medical profession.

He pushed the bottle of pills across the table. 'What do you think of these? Are they any good?'

Lara read the label. 'Duractin. Chemically that's cimetidine. Very effective in healing gastric ulcers.' She paused and frowned at her boss. 'You're supposed to take them with meals, and at bedtime. I suppose you didn't have any lunch?'

'Didn't have time,' he grunted. Then, rebelliously, 'So what's the difference? I'm taking 'em.'

'Some drugs act more efficiently and cause less side-effects if taken with food,' Lara said. 'If it says three times a day with meals there's a good reason for it. How long have you been taking these?'

'Coupla' weeks.'

'Any improvement?'

He suppressed a burp. 'No. It still gives me gyp. In between meals I keep the antacid boys in business!' He toyed with a packet of antacid tablets as though debating whether to take one or not.

Lara passed the bottle of Duractin back to him. 'It might take a few weeks to show any improvement. I'm not your physician, Grant. I can't diagnose or treat you, but I can say that if you don't take your medication according to instructions, and if you don't ease up a bit and let other people worry—in other words, delegate more—then you're going to be in for a rough time.

You'll end up hospitalised and someone else will have to worry about *New Era* whether you like it or not.'

'God! You nag just like my wife!' Grant roared, and his laughter exploded round the room. 'Wives and doctors—worst pessimists in the world.'

'Wrong, Grant,' said Lara with a smile. 'Doctors are optimists. Otherwise we wouldn't keep trying to keep body-abusers like you on the straight and narrow.'

'"*We*"?' he queried with a raised eyebrow. 'You're not a doctor now!'

'A slip of the tongue,' Lara said, and collected a speculative look from her boss. Then he glared at her fiercely for a moment, and she thought she'd gone too far criticising him. But at last he relaxed. 'You're a cheeky young journo,' he said with a sudden grin. 'Nobody could put much past you, could they? How's it going with Dirk? Have you put him out of his misery yet?'

Lara blushed. 'There's nothing going with Dirk.'

'That's not what Dirk says,' said Grant bluntly. 'He only needs a nod to park his shoes under your bed.'

'I don't often nod!'

He laughed and leaned back in his chair. He looked, Lara thought, almost relaxed. It was a pity he couldn't be like this more often. She knew it wouldn't last.

'OK, sweetheart, keep up the good work,' Grant said. 'I'll take a look at this later.' He stuffed her disk into a holder on his desk near his personal word-processor, and swivelled round to face the main VDU he had been working at when she'd entered.

Lara rose and left, a little worried about him. He was obviously pushing himself too hard to make the paper hold its position among the rash of new Sundays that had erupted into Melbourne's weekend during the past couple of years. At thirty he could have stood the pace, but at fifty he could not expect to be so resilient. He had too many liquid lunches and was overweight. She was, in fact, more anxious about his arteries than his ulcer. It was just as well he'd shifted from the daily paper where he'd been chief of staff, but *New Era* was proving to be not quite the rest cure his long-suffering wife had once confided to Lara that she had hoped for.

Lara was reading through the latest batch of mail she'd received as a result of her recent article on new advances in prosthetic design when Dirk Hoeskstra came in.

'Hi, Caro. You look pleased with yourself.'

'Just reading my fan mail!' She grinned at him, adding seriously, 'Some people are so cheerful about things like artificial legs and arms. I don't know if I could be so philosophical and optimistic.'

Dirk shuddered. 'Nor me, but I guess you cope when you have to.' He leaned over closer to her. 'You look very sexy today. Know what I'd like to do?'

'Take pictures of me in the nude? For art's sake? That's what you said yesterday.' Lara smiled sweetly. 'No way!'

'No, today I feel a little more ambitious and less arty. . .' Dirk drawled in a sexy tone.

She shook her finger at him. 'Haven't you got anything better to do than chat up the female staff?'

'Only you, darling,' Dirk said, trying to get his mouth closer to hers. 'Only you drive me wild!'

Lara dodged the kiss he was intent on. 'Grant's in there giving himself ulcers over, quote, "our layabout photographers", end of quote.'

Dirk hunched his knees up and hugged them. 'I'm waiting for something to happen—a fire, or an earthquake,' he said, deadpan.

'Ghoul! Anyway, you're on a weekly now, Dirk,' Lara reminded him. 'Not so much scope for scoops. And please take those disgusting boots off my desk!'

He yawned. 'What about this new series you're doing? Am I taking the pics?'

'I thought you were squeamish about hospitals,' Lara laughed, 'but I can pull strings if you want.'

Dirk leapt off the desk and masterfully pulled her out of her chair into his arms. 'What I really want, Caro. . .'

I suppose I ought to tell him about my name, Lara thought, dodging his mouth again, since if he does come with me later he's going to think it very odd when everyone at the hospital calls me by my real name.

'Give over, Dirk,' she said, squirming away from him. 'And, while I think of it, there's a small matter to clear up. Caroline Kelly is my pseudonym. My real name is Lara Montague. It was easier to use my pseudonym all the time, but a guy I used to know has turned up in the cardiac surgery department at South City General and he's let the cat out of the bag. I thought I'd better mention it.'

'Lara?' Dirk looked taken aback. 'You mean I've got to call you Lara? What sort of a fancy monicker is that? No wonder you changed it.'

'It's a perfectly good name and I like it. But you don't have to use it. In fact, I'd rather you went on calling me Caro, and you needn't spread it all over the office that it's a pseudonym.'

'What are you hiding, Caro?' Dirk asked, only half teasing.

'Nothing! Lots of people use pseudonyms, especially medicos who write.'

He looked at her oddly, and for a moment Lara had a sinking feeling that a bell was ringing in his memory. . .that his mind was going back several years. . .that a tiny suspicion might send him to the files. No—*New Era*'s files didn't go back that far. . .the newspaper hadn't existed even two years ago. But Dirk had worked for other papers and would be able to get access to their files. Well, he would only find that she'd been completely exonerated. Careful, she cautioned herself, you're being paranoid.

'How about dinner tonight?' Dirk suggested. 'There's a new place just opened up near the beach at St Kilda.'

Lara would normally have said yes. She enjoyed Dirk's breezy company, and, although it usually meant fending off too-heavy amorous advances, she always enjoyed herself with him. But for once she didn't want to go out with him. She didn't know why.

'Will it keep?' she said. 'I've got some urgent work to do tonight.'

'Your hair doesn't need washing; it looks fine!'

Lara laughed. 'No, but I want to do some research into heart surgery, for background, and I've got an appointment at the SCG library at three-thirty, which means I'd better move because I'm probably going to have a lot of photocopying to do.'

Lara spent an hour in the library with a very helpful librarian, who eagerly looked up for her every bit of information she could find on bypass operations and transplants and all the latest experimental techniques.

The photocopier ran hot as Lara took stats of what she
wanted to peruse at leisure.

As soon as she had finished in the library she went up
to the cardiac surgery department. The lift stopped at
the next floor and Teresa Ioannidis got in.

'Oh—good afternoon, Dr Montague,' Teresa said
coolly.

'Lara, please,' said Lara. She added, 'How's the
judge?'

'Still in Intensive Care, but stable.' Sister Ioannidis's
answers were clipped, cool, reluctant. Just short of being
hostile.

'Is Lucas in?'

Teresa's eyes flickered dangerously, and her mouth
contracted a little as she said tightly, 'Yes, I think so.'
The lift doors opened and she sailed out without another
word.

Lara continued to the floor above. Reception rang
through to Lucas for her, and then one of the receptionists showed her into his office.

He rose from his desk as she entered, and for a
moment Lara wished she hadn't come. Their passionate
encounter yesterday was still too vividly in her mind,
and her reactions to him were very definitely contra-
indications. Lucas Turnbull was proving to be even
more of a lethal drug now than he had before, a drug
which was destroying her peace of mind.

'Lara. . .come in. Sit down. I wasn't expecting you.'

He was smoothly professional, even distant, as though
she were no more than an acquaintance or a colleague
he didn't know very well. He looked devastating none
the less, and her knees felt weak.

'I hope I'm not interrupting anything. I should have made an appointment.'

'No problem.' Lucas watched her sink into a chair and tried for an air of complete detachment, but the memory of her warm body tantalisingly close to his, of her mouth, her breasts, her surprising responsiveness, were so much closer in the time scale now—only a day ago instead of a decade—so much more vivid, and he still wanted her. Was that just because she'd frustrated him, he wondered, or was he falling into her trap all over again? He tightened his mouth, crammed a lid on his emotions, and tried again for clinical detachment. She'd played hard to get before, but that was understandable then; she'd been only nineteen. Was she doing the same now for different reasons? He'd better be careful. She'd have no compunction about picking him up and dropping him again when she felt inclined. She was a career woman, and he'd better remember that. If he ever did get her into bed he'd better remember it well. He'd better be sure not to let his feelings become involved. He mustn't be fool enough to let her make him suffer again.

'You look annoyed with me,' Lara said, perturbed by his lengthy silence.

'I was just thinking how chic you look,' Lucas said with a slightly twisted grin. 'Black and white suits you. Very businesslike.' And very sexy, he thought.

Lara glanced down at the black and white houndstooth-check suit she was wearing with its crisp white jacket revers and slim skirt. 'Thanks.' She went on, 'I came to look up a few things in the library, so while I was here I thought I'd call up and see how Mr Justice Allardyce is progressing.'

His expression relaxed a fraction. 'And I thought you'd come to see me.'

She was glad to see he was thawing. 'Don't kid yourself, Lucas,' she replied, not altogether joking.

He walked round the desk and stood looking down at her. God, she was good to look at. Something in her eyes set the pulses racing, and that faint dimple near the left side of her mouth was still so damn tantalising. And she was still spirited. That was what had attracted him to her most in the first place. She had a sense of humour too, and a sharp wit. And yet she could also be so kind, like the other day when she'd ironed his suit without a murmur. Other women he knew, not half so clever, would have turned up their noses at ironing his crumpled suit. Not many would have made him breakfast, and he doubted if any would have still offered him lunch after he'd overstepped the line and they'd given him the brush-off. Not that he was used to getting the brush-off. The trouble was it only made him want her more. . .

'Would you like to see him?'

'I'd like to interview him when he's out of IC,' Lara said. 'That is if he's willing.'

He lifted a dark eyebrow. 'The human interest bit?'

She wished he weren't so cynical about her work. 'Well, you are dealing with people. Hearts are not piston engines.'

Lucas laughed. She'd always had a quick answer. He wished she didn't look so damn kissable. When she was on the defensive she made a man yearn to soften her. . .especially when he knew how soft she really was. . .

'I hope I have never lost sight of the fact that patients

are human beings,' he said, and a barely perceptible muscle movement beside his mouth betrayed emotion.

Lara regretted her implied criticism. 'I didn't mean you had. But you're so scathing about my job.'

'Am I?' He was surprised.

'Sometimes it certainly sounds like it. I have the feeling you regard me as some sort of traitor to the medical profession.'

'I'm sorry. Perhaps it's just that I'm disappointed that you quit being a doctor.' He paused, then added pointedly, 'You were so dedicated once. It was your whole life.'

'People change, Lucas,' Lara said. 'I was nineteen and starry-eyed about medicine, but life turned up other opportunities. We all have to make decisions some time or other.'

His eyes were penetrating. 'And you've never regretted any of yours?'

'No,' she said firmly, refusing to acknowledge the doubts that seemed to be plaguing her more and more lately. She sighed. 'Can't you just accept that I like my job? You've agreed to help me do my series on heart surgery, and I'd like to make another request.'

'Go ahead.'

'I'd very much like to interview a patient before an operation, Lucas, if you could arrange it,' Lara said boldly.

He folded his arms in a characteristic gesture across his chest. 'I'll see.' He wasn't going to capitulate too easily. She might get the idea she could wrap him around her little finger. 'All this is, of course, on one condition.'

Lara was mildly alarmed. He hadn't mentioned conditions before. 'What's that?'

'I want to see what you write. Everything.'

She was taken aback. 'You want to approve the copy? Lucas, I'm not sure. . .'

He was adamant. 'I think I have a right to ask that.'

Lara chewed her bottom lip. 'All right.'

There was a small silence to emphasise the point, then Lucas said amiably, 'I was about to go and see Judge Allardyce myself. You can come if you like. You might as well, now you're here.'

Lara smiled at him. 'All right, I will. Thanks.' As they walked along the corridor to the intensive care unit, she asked, 'What are his chances, Lucas?'

'Fair,' the surgeon answered. 'Like far too many people, he hasn't been treating his body kindly, and a lot will depend on how he treats it in future.'

'But he's recovering from the op OK?'

'So far, so good,' Lucas said cautiously. 'He's not out of the woods yet, obviously, but let's say, off the record. . .' he smiled sidelong at her '. . . I'm quietly confident.'

Judge Allardyce, surrounded by life-support equipment and still sprouting a couple of tubes, was asleep. Looking at the pale round face of the lawyer, Lara found it hard to imagine him in court, bewigged and authoritarian. Here, prostrate between stark white sheets, he looked vulnerable. Illness, she thought, was a great leveller.

Lara kept her distance and let her eyes absorb the details of the room and the patient in the bed, the nurse monitoring the array of high-tech equipment. Lucas engaged the woman in low conversation and examined charts and graphs, nodding occasionally. He made a short personal examination of the patient and then motioned Lara closer.

'No problems,' he told her with satisfaction.

As they went out of the room Lara commented, 'It's very rewarding to be able to save lives, isn't it?'

Lucas gave her a sharp look. 'Envious?'

Lara bit her lip. She'd asked for the barb. 'Medicine has its down side too. It isn't all success, honour and glory.'

'No,' Lucas answered in a tone that sounded so meaningful that Lara looked quickly up into his face. She caught a flicker of pain there, as she had once before, that made her wonder again if there weren't something that had happened to Lucas, the memory of which was never far below the surface.

'I'd better be going,' she said as they neared the lifts. 'Thanks for everything, Lucas.' She gave him a pert look. 'And I'll make sure you see the final copy— although I can't guarantee the subs won't mangle it afterwards.'

He caught hold of her hand, enveloping it tightly in his large one. 'Shall we see if we can get a full meal in tonight?'

Lara's heart fluttered a bit, but she said, 'Thanks, but I want to get on with my background research.' She tapped her briefcase. 'I've got some reading to do.'

'You might have a lot of questions,' he said. 'I could bring a pizza round to your place.'

She frowned at him. 'Look what happened the last time you came to my place.'

'I promise not to fall asleep on your couch.'

'That wasn't what I meant!'

He lifted her hand to his lips and touched her knuckles

briefly. The contact sent a tingling sensation along her veins. 'I promise to be good. . .' His eyes met hers with a mischievous glint.

'You are an incorrigible flirt,' Lara said. 'No—worse! You are an indefatigable seducer! But I'm not a starry-eyed med student any more, you know. Superior surgeons, however sexy, don't sweep me off my feet any more. Try your luck somewhere else.' Teresa's more than willing, Lara was tempted to add. But maybe the Greek girl wasn't available until the weekend.

'Was that all it was?' Lucas said, dropping her hand. 'A passing fancy?'

'I was nineteen, Lucas. I didn't know my own mind. I was flattered by your attention. I got carried away by the glamour of falling in love with a surgeon years older than I was.' She paused and said impatiently, 'It's all been said before, Lucas. There's no point in going over it again. I'm sorry, I truly am, for what I did. I can only plead youth, naïveté——'

'Don't go on,' he said roughly, and in a sudden gesture pulled her against him, holding her head against his chest. 'You don't have to apologise. Oh, Lara. . .'

Fortunately the corridor was for a moment deserted and no one saw the cardiac surgery department's director embracing the journalist from *New Era*. He pushed her away as abruptly as he had held her and said savagely, 'Don't worry, I'm not likely to make a fool of myself over you a second time!'

He pushed the 'down' button for her. 'Enjoy your research, Lara. I'll be in touch when there's anything worth your observing.'

Shaken by the intensity of emotion she sensed beneath

his apparently perfect control, Lara said, 'Thanks again. See you. . .soon.'

The lift bell rang as the lift arrived, but Lucas was striding off down the corridor to his office without a backward look before she had even entered it. She had hurt his pride more than she had ever realised, Lara now knew. He wanted to punish her for that. That was why he had tried to make love to her the other night. He had wanted to prove that he could still sweep her off her feet.

That he still could was a realisation Lara was unwilling to contemplate, and one she must be careful never to let Lucas discover. He would be careful not to make a fool of himself again, he'd said. But he wouldn't baulk at making a fool of her.

CHAPTER FIVE

WHEN a fortnight passed and there was no word from Lucas, no call to the hospital, Lara decided that Lucas had changed his mind after all and did not intend to let her observe any more heart surgery.

She had no alternative but to believe that he had only agreed in the first place because he wanted to keep in touch with her for a time so that he could execute his own personal revenge, and when he failed to seduce her that put an end to it. Evidently he expected her to realise that.

Even so, there were times when Lara wanted to pick up the phone and ask him what the score was, but she couldn't seem to find the nerve. Not even when Grant was on her back to get moving on the series. He'd liked her first piece and was clamouring for more.

Rattling his bottle of pills, he'd barked, 'What's the matter with them? Aren't they doing any life-saving operations any more?'

His expression brought a fleeting smile to Lara's face, and, despite her misgivings about Lucas's intentions, she prevaricated. 'Of course they are, but what we want if possible is the unusual. I've written up a quadruple bypass, so I need to wait until something different comes up.' She pointed a finger at him. 'You wouldn't wish illness on people just so you could get your series on time, would you?'

He rolled his eyes at the ceiling. 'You'll never make a journalist, kid.'

'I thought I was one!'

He chuckled. 'Lady, you're a talented writer, but you've got too big a heart for a real journo. We're a tough breed. We don't get involved. You ought to have stuck to doctoring, my girl. I don't know why you fiddle around writing about it when you could be doing it, but I'm glad you do. Your material is good. The follow-up piece you did on the judge was terrific. With a bit of luck you'll win a Walkley Award this time.'

'Thanks,' Lara said drily. His rough perception was a little too close to the truth for comfort. 'Mr Justice Allardyce was very co-operative. He's willing to talk to me again in a few weeks for a progress report.'

'You know how to get 'em talking,' Grant conceded. 'I suppose that's a gift that helps make good journos and good quacks.'

'What did your "quack" tell you about Duractin?' Lara enquired silkily.

Grant answered grudgingly, 'Same as you did, blast him! I think I'll go to a naturopath.'

Lara laughed. 'You'll probably get very similar advice, even if the tablets are different.' She added, only half seriously, 'Want an article on naturopathy while I'm hanging about?'

He peered over his steel-rimmed spectacles. 'Hey, that's a great idea! Alternative medicine. Look into it, Lara. Get the historical perspective, and the conventional medicine viewpoint. Professional rivalry. Who are the real quacks? Yeah—it's got possibilities. Wasn't the government going to bring in strict regulations that the natural therapies people said would put them out of business? Don't quote me. Better check the files on that. . .'

Lara was no longer astonished at the decisiveness with which Grant could adopt an idea or throw one out. More than once he'd declared derisively, 'Rubbish! No story in that, girl!' to her tentative suggestions. He was usually right.

'I'll draft a proposal,' she said. It was strange how ideas sometimes came right out of the blue, or were sparked off by a chance remark.

For a few days Lara thought of little else but her new project. It was a whole new experience delving into natural therapies, and Lara found it fascinating, although her conventional medical training meant she was conditioned by a degree of scepticism. She drafted a proposal and Grant approved her plan of approach. He told her in his usual brusque fashion—on a day when his ulcer was troubling him more than usual—to 'stop messing about and get on with it, girl!'

Although she feared it was futile, and that she would have to confront Grant with the reality soon, Lara still waited patiently for her telephone to ring to summon her to South City General, and when she went into the office the first thing she did was check her messages, but still there was nothing. She was reluctant to face up to the loss of what had appeared to be a great journalistic opportunity, but even harder was forcing herself to believe that she was never going to see or speak to Lucas again. That her greater disappointment was over this shocked her, and the gnawing ache it induced was something she had never expected to experience.

Lara threw herself into the natural-therapies project with deliberate gusto, but her enthusiasm was forced and her mind kept straying back to the cardiac surgery series, which she tried to believe was only 'on hold', and—although she denied it to herself—just as often to Lucas. She would give it another week, she decided, before she told Grant, which wouldn't be easy. The week passed, nothing happened, and she knew she could not put off the evil hour any longer.

Lara was mulling it all over in her mind very dispiritedly one afternoon when she was heading back to the office after lunch with an extremely garrulous iridologist. The woman had been extraordinarily persuasive, but Lara was not entirely convinced of the efficacy of diagnosis by examination of the eyes, although as always she was keeping the open mind necessary to writing unbiased articles. I'd better tell Grant, she decided at last, her mind skipping easily from iridology to cardiology, as she went up in the lift. I'd better put him in the picture.

It was with a deep sense of her own failure that Lara went straight along to Grant's office, but she was not to be required to deliver her hastily rehearsed speech because Grant was in no position to receive it.

'Lara!' A voice hailed her as she turned into the corridor where the *New Era*'s deputy editor had his office. It was the chief of staff, Tony Fleming. He ran towards her. 'Lara, quick! It's Grant. He's had a heart attack—I think. You're a doctor. Maybe you can help. . .' He pushed a hand distractedly through already rumpled hair. 'Jill's rung the ambulance.'

Lara's personal thoughts scattered as she ran the few yards along the corridor to her boss's office. Half a dozen others were standing around an inert figure on the floor looking scared and helpless.

Lara flung her briefcase and handbag into a chair and fell to her knees by the still form of Grant Jermyn. She swiftly checked his eyes and pulse, then glanced up. 'How long ago did he collapse?'

Everyone turned to Jill, his secretary, who was crying. 'How long ago, Jill?' Lara repeated urgently.

'Not long—only a few minutes,' Jill said. 'I—I was with him when he just gave a terrible groan and collapsed. I—I thought it must be a heart attack, so I rushed out and rang for an ambulance.'

'Has anyone tried to revive him?' Lara demanded. 'Mouth-to-mouth? Heart massage?'

She was greeted by blank looks. When it came to a real crisis all those charts on the office walls explaining how to resuscitate a heart-attack victim were so often forgotten. Lara did not waste any more time. She feared it was already too late to save Grant—the blueness around his lips, the dilated pupils and absence of pulse indicated that his heart had stopped. But she had to try. By the time the ambulance arrived with resuscitation equipment it might be too late. Even if they were able to revive him, he might suffer irreparable brain damage. She was aware that he might have suffered that already, but she didn't want Grant to die, and if it was only a few minutes since he'd collapsed. . .

Lara gently but firmly dismissed all those who were not necessary, and within seconds she had Tony working on respiration while she started compressions on Grant's chest. It was a long time since she had resuscitated anyone or even demonstrated on a model, but, as she placed the heel of her hand on the correct spot on the sternum and locked her other hand around her wrist, the rhythm asserted itself.

'One inflation to five compressions,' she said to Tony, who nodded tensely.

He was calm, competent and obeyed her instructions to the letter. Lara guessed he'd learned the drill some time and she was thankful for that.

For a full minute they worked on the deputy editor with intense concentration. Why doesn't the ambulance get here? Lara kept thinking. The first time she paused to check the carotid pulse there was no sign of it. After another minute she felt a flutter of life and drew an exultant breath as she caught Tony's eye. 'He's coming back,' she breathed, hoping fervently they could keep him coming. 'Keep going. . .'

'Hang in there, Grant, old man,' Tony whispered, and continued to inflate the deputy editor's chest after every five compressions. When Lara's fingers on the patient's neck satisfied her that there was a definite pulse in the carotid artery, she ceased heart massage and took over from Tony for a few inflations. She was at the point of exhaustion when a flurry of activity announced the arrival of the ambulance team, which had been delayed in a traffic jam. Within seconds the manual resuscitation had been taken over by sophisticated mechanical equipment. Lara held her breath as she watched Grant's colour change and become more normal. She heaved a sigh of relief.

Tony smiled at her. 'Just as well you arrived when you did. He's going to pull through, isn't he?'

She nodded wearily, a frown creasing her brow. 'I hope so. I just hope we weren't too. . .too tardy, that's all.'

'You mean brain damage?' Tony looked worried.

Lara nodded.

The chief of staff squeezed her hand. 'He's a tough guy, Lara. He'll be all right. Lucky for him there was a doctor in the house!'

One of the ambulance paramedics said to Lara, 'You're a doctor?'

'I was. . . I mean, I am but I haven't practised for a few years. I'm a journalist. . .medical journalist.'

'Maybe you should come along with us,' the man suggested, 'since you were here and know what happened.' He glanced around. 'Somebody'd better notify his next of kin.'

Lara agreed. To Jill she said, 'You'd better ring his wife, Jill.'

The girl nodded, calm now, although pale. She went out to her office. Lara gripped the chief's arm. 'Keep your fingers crossed, Tony.'

He clasped a hand over hers. 'You bet!' He accompanied her down to the ambulance and helped load the stretcher.

For a little while Lara almost forgot she was no longer a practising doctor. The ambulancemen treated her as one, and so did the casualty staff at the hospital. So concerned was she about Grant's condition that the possibility of her seeing Lucas as a result of the crisis did not even impinge on her mind until he suddenly appeared.

Lucas had been studying some angiogram reports when he'd been alerted to the emergency, but his mind had not been as fully occupied with the task in hand as it might have been. As was happening all too often nowadays, he found himself thinking about Lara. He had decided to renege on his promise to let her observe more operations because seeing her was too disturbing, but it bothered him that he had not made it clear. Just letting the matter drift was not like him. Maybe she'd got the message, but nevertheless it bothered him. *She* bothered him. . .

Several times he'd reached for the phone to call her and apologise, to make some excuse, but each time had faltered. To speak to her would only churn his emotions up all over again. Better to let it slide, to let her assume what was in fact the case—that he did not want to see her again. But the trouble was he *did* want to see her again, and fighting it was turning him into a 'bear with a sore head', as one irritated colleague had remarked.

There was an antidote, of course. Other women. If he was to forget Lara, he must occupy himself with other women. . . Lucas was contemplating the possibilities when the red alert sounded and he hotfooted it to the casualty department. Seeing Lara there was as though he were hallucinating.

'It's Grant,' she said, a wave of thankfulness sweeping over her at the sight of him. At his puzzled look she added, 'Grant Jermyn, my boss. He's had a heart attack.' She smiled grimly. 'It's hardly surprising the way he drives himself. He's also got an ulcer. . .' Suddenly the shock that she too had suffered seeing someone she liked and admired apparently dead surfaced, and she choked on her words as tears started to stream down her face. She turned her face away, not wanting Lucas to see.

He touched her shoulder. 'Take it easy, Lara.'

She turned back. 'I'm OK. It happened at the office and I came along to give what information I can since I know him pretty well.'

Lucas gave her a sharp look. 'Yes, I suppose you do.'

Sensing an innuendo, Lara said stiffly, 'His wife will be here any minute. If there's anything else they need to know. . .'

Lara stayed to see Nora Jermyn and long enough to hear that Grant would need bypass surgery. She comforted Nora as best she could.

'He's in good hands,' she assured her. 'Lucas Turnbull is a first-rate surgeon and he runs a top team.'

Nora had heard the details of her husband's collapse and she pressed Lara's hands in hers gratefully. 'What you did for him. . .' she said tearfully. 'Lara. . .if you hadn't been there. . .if you hadn't been a doctor and able to. . .'

'Don't talk about it,' Lara murmured. 'It's all over now and he's going to be all right. I'm sure he is.' She wasn't, but she could say nothing less to the distraught Nora.

A few days later Lara visited Grant in hospital. Her worst fears had not been realised. He had survived surgery and there was no apparent brain damage from the delay before resuscitation after his heart attack. He was still in Intensive Care, but awake. His usual dynamism and abrasiveness were muted by relaxant drugs, but he had not lost his dry humour.

'Dragged me back from the grave, I hear,' he accused with a grin. 'Thought you'd have been glad to see me pass over!'

'*New Era* couldn't manage without you,' she retorted. 'And I'm glad to see you still seem to have all your brain cells! But you'll have to take it a bit easier, Grant, if you don't want a repeat performance. I might not always be around to shatter your ribs.'

'Doc says you didn't,' he stated. 'Pretty good heart massager, by all accounts.' He gave her a long look. 'Wouldn't you rather be a doctor than a journalist?'

'No.'

'I don't believe you,' he stated flatly, then demanded, 'Tell me what's going on at the office.'

'Business as usual. We can get on without you, Grant. Not as well, perhaps, but we get by. . .'

He grunted sceptically. 'I'd like to know what's holding up your heart-surgery series.' He pulled a face. 'Did you do a piece on me?'

'We sketched out an obit!' Lara laughed. 'Just in case. But your op was too ordinary to write up,' she teased, 'too run of the mill, Grant, to interest the readers. Not much drama really.'

'Enough for me,' he said in an uncharacteristically quiet tone. 'And Nora.' He was thoughtful for a moment, then said, 'Maybe I'd better have a word with this Turnbull fellow about your series.'

Lara said quickly, 'No, don't, Grant. I'm not sure he wants me to continue. He doesn't really like observers. . .'

'But you haven't got enough copy yet for the series we planned. He can't go back on his word, damn him!'

Lara tried to soothe him. 'You mustn't worry about it, Grant. I'll talk to Lucas—let me handle it. You mustn't get involved in office problems while you're convalescing.'

He grunted again, obviously reluctant to relinquish the reins completely, despite his brush with death. Some men were just like that, Lara knew, and nothing would change them. Unless a miracle happened and he changed his outlook and lifestyle, one day Grant would have an attack that would be fatal.

Lara was glad to see Nora walk in, as seeing his wife was bound to distract Grant from work. 'I'll be going,' she said, and quietly slipped out of the room, only to walk practically into the arms of Lucas.

He looked her over with swift assessment. 'Hello, Lara.'

'Hello, Lucas. I was just having a few words with Grant.' She knew her colour was up, and feeling its warmth made it worse. Just seeing Lucas, just being inches away from him made her skin tingle and shivers run along her spine. 'Nora's with him now,' she said.

'So you made a hasty exit,' Lucas commented. He was blocking her route to the lifts and seemed disinclined to let her rush past him.

'Not hasty. . .but one visitor at a time, I think. . .'

'In the circumstances, naturally.'

Lucas's gaze was steady, searching her face, and Lara had no difficulty reading his mind. The implication incensed her. 'What circumstances precisely?'

'You were pretty upset the other day when it happened.'

'Certainly I was. Grant's my boss.'

'Is that all?'

Lara felt a strong desire to hit the man. 'How dare you?'

He was unmoved. 'I gather you saved his life with some pretty effective CPR.'

'I did what needed to be done. I would have done the same for anyone.'

'I'm not suggesting you wouldn't have. You are a doctor, after all.'

Lucas laid heavy emphasis on the last remark, and Lara flinched. A silence developed until Lara wondered why she was still standing there. 'I'd better be going,' she said, making a move to walk past him, then she paused. Surely now was the moment to tackle him about observing future operations, to settle the matter once and for all? She gathered her courage and steeled herself for the expected rebuff, but was neatly foiled by the sudden appearance of a nurse in a hurry, wanting Lucas.

'Excuse me. . .' he murmured, and Lara was left standing in the corridor as his white-coated figure strode with the nurse into the distance.

Well, so what? she thought resignedly. I'd probably only have made a fool of myself. He's as good as told me it's all off, so what's the point in harassing him about it? She walked slowly along to the lifts and hoped that Grant would not bring up the subject with Lucas. He would not succeed and it would only cause Grant frustration.

A few days later Lara was at home working, had just glanced at the time—six-thirty p.m.—which made her realise how hungry she was, and was about to get up and make a snack meal for herself, when the doorbell pealed. She opened it to Lucas Turnbull bearing a large flat cardboard box.

'Lucas! What. . .?' The sight of him again caused her heart to race and the colour to flood her cheeks. It infuriated her that she could be so vulnerable.

He glanced down in mock anxiety. 'What's up? Are my flies undone?'

'What?'

'You're blushing.'

'Oh, really!' Lara exclaimed, dissolving into laughter. After the rather grim tone of their previous encounter, his light-heartedness was unexpected and she was taken aback. Caught off guard, and somewhat perplexed, she took refuge in being facetious. 'Why don't you grow up, Mr Turnbull, and behave more in keeping with your station in life?' She pointed to the box. 'And what, may I ask, is that?'

'A full set of organs, specially preserved for your dissection.' He pushed past her into the hall and staggered slightly. Lara realised why he was being so flippant.

'Don't be so disgusting! You're drunk,' she accused.

He grinned lop-sidedly. 'Maybe just a little bit tipsy. . .but food will fix it.' He thrust the box into her arms. 'Pop it in the microwave, there's a dear girl.' He then withdrew from a very tight fit in his jacket pocket a bottle of wine, which he waved about in a rather alarming fashion.

'I think you'd better go and sit down in the living-room and I'll make you some black coffee,' Lara said, half amused, half dismayed. She glanced at the label on the box. 'Tower of Pisa Pizza House—Family-Size Gourmet.' Lucas was still grinning at her foolishly and his look was so endearing that Lara felt choked. This was shades of the Lucas she had known years ago and it was very disconcerting.

She gave him a push. 'Go on—in there.'   Lucas stumbled into the living-room and flung himself down on the couch. Lara hurried off to the kitchen and switched on the coffee percolator, then put some crackers on a plate for him to be going on with. She was laughing in spite of herself. He'd looked so silly, hair all awry, eyes glazed, and trying to get that bottle out of his pocket! What on earth had he been up to?

Lucas slumped when she'd gone. He began to feel uncomfortably sober after all. He shouldn't have come. He'd spent two hours in a bar trying to make up his mind whether to phone Lara or go and see her, and he'd finally got intoxicated enough to persuade himself to go in person and to take a large gourmet pizza, not caring if he got the brush-off or if she did have another fellow there.

Lara brought him a cup of coffee and some crackers. 'Here, eat these and drink your coffee while I heat the pizza,' she ordered.

He gave her a silly smile. She looked good enough to eat herself. The black sweater clinging to her luscious curves and the short mustard skirt that showed off her lovely legs were enough to set any red-blooded male's pulse pounding. 'Thanks,' he said.

'And don't fall asleep!' she cautioned.

Lucas chuckled. 'I'll try not to.' He asked hastily, 'Have you eaten already?'

She shook her head. 'As a matter of fact, I haven't. I was working so hard that I forgot the time. I was just about to make a snack when you rang the bell.'

'So I arrived like a gift from heaven.'

'More like a bolt from the blue,' she said drily.

'You don't mind?'

Lara gritted her teeth. 'Of course not. But perhaps you could have rung first. . .'

'Because you might have had company, been going out. . .Yes, I did think of a number of possibilities, but— well, considering everything, you might have put me off anyway, so I thought I'd risk it.'

'Excuse me,' Lara said. 'I'll just heat the pizza and toss some salad. I won't be long. Switch the television on if you want.'

Lucas sighed as she departed. He'd been afraid she might throw him out. He wasn't even sure why he was there at all. It was partly from some deep-rooted desire to punish her even more by telling her he'd changed his mind and he wouldn't even agree to her publishing her first article, and yet as soon as he saw her that was the last thing on his mind. Or had he expected to catch her with a male visitor?

So what was the point? He surely didn't expect she was likely to let *him* seduce her? If his ego had imagined that, in the absence of other men friends, she just might this time, then the sight of her face as he'd come in was enough to convince him that vanity reaped its own punishment. He reminded himself that he hadn't exactly endeared himself to Lara lately. But she hadn't thrown him out yet, and the thought of an evening with Lara, eating pizza and drinking wine and talking, was an attractive one, one to override all other considerations. All his perverse thoughts about continuing to obstruct her deserted him. He gulped down the coffee and munched the crackers while watching the TV news, and felt his head clear.

Lara came back to announce that the meal was ready. 'I don't know whether you should have the wine,' she said doubtfully.

He stood up, clicking his heels together. 'Perfectly sober now, Dr Montague,' he said.

'You've been drinking on an empty stomach, I sup-pose,' she accused.

'A foolish thing to do,' he said. 'I was drowning my sorrows.'

'Who with?' Lara asked. 'Was she blonde or brunette, and did she slap your face when you got fresh so that you decided to come and annoy me instead?'

Involuntarily he touched her hair, stroking it back from her temple. 'Why are you so hard, Lara?' he said softly. Then, half teasingly, 'I wasn't with anyone. There's no need to be jealous.'

She shrugged away from him. 'Jealous? Huh! That'll be the day. Come and eat, before it gets cold.' His touch was still making her nerve-ends tingle. She wished she knew why he had come.

He trailed after her back to the kitchen. 'I'll open the wine. It's a genuine Italian Chianti.'

'I'm impressed,' Lara said drily, tossing him a bottle-opener.

He frowned reproachfully. 'You're being very sharp.'

He was right—she was, Lara thought. It was because he'd taken her by surprise and she didn't know whether she welcomed him or wished he hadn't come. Her feelings were not at all clear. When she wasn't in contact with him she was sure she had Lucas Turnbull in proper perspective, but seeing him standing outside her door, smiling in that silly tipsy way, holding out the family-size pizza, had opened a strange hollow in her stomach. She had never quite got him out of her system, she realised. She had jilted him, but he had never quite gone away from her.

She said, 'You took me by surprise. And I'm always wary of men who've had too much to drink.'

He laughed softly. 'I promise I won't try to violate

your honour, Dr Montague. I got a flea in my ear last time. I'm a quick learner, you know.'

Lara felt her annoyance being charmed away. He had as much charisma as he'd ever had, and she was still vulnerable—to a degree anyway. It was one of the things she'd liked about him in the beginning, she recalled: his lack of stuffiness. He'd never strutted around as some surgeons she knew had, never regarded himself as some sort of exalted being way above the heads of mere interns and medical students. He'd been a good demonstrator, patient with them, willing to answer any question, however naïve. She'd learned a lot from him—and not only medical expertise, she thought with sudden wistfulness as she watched him extract the cork from the bottle with a satisfying pop. She fetched two wine glasses and placed them on the table.

'Pizza smells good,' remarked Lucas as she opened the oven door.

'Did you realise it's a family size?' Lara asked, amused.

'Yes. And don't bank on having any left-overs for tomorrow. I'm starving. I didn't have any lunch.'

'You're as bad as Grant. You ought to have lunch, and you ought to know that better than anyone. What use is a surgeon with ulcers or cardiac disease?'

He grinned at her and drawled, 'You sound as though you care!'

Lara pursed her lips. 'Doctors are trained to, aren't they?' She cut the pizza into slices and lifted one on to his plate. 'Help yourself to salad.'

'I wonder what it'd be like being a patient of Dr Montague's,' Lucas mused, grinding pepper over his meal. 'Pity she gave it up. She's got a lovely bedside manner.' He looked across at her, but he wasn't smiling. 'Even Grant Jermyn says so.'

Lara wished he would stop needling her about her career change. She lifted her wine glass. 'Cheers!' She sipped the deep-red Chianti. 'Mm, that's nice.' She went on, 'Now, tell me what brings you here. I assume there was a reason.'

'I've got a case for you.' The words were spoken before he realised it. Perhaps it was why he had come after all, because he'd felt guilty about promising her something and then letting her down. That Jermyn fellow had made him feel a heel. He wondered if Lara had put Grant up to tackling him, but thought not. She wouldn't have done that; not while the man was ill.

Lara's eyes widened in amazement. 'I thought you'd changed your mind. I thought. . .well, as you haven't contacted me for weeks. . .'

'I was waiting for something worthwhile to come up,' he said blandly, astonished at his own deviousness, and ignoring his perversity.

Lara was astute. 'I suppose Grant's been getting at you.' She felt some annoyance at this.

'He mentioned the series and naturally wondered why you seemed to be held up. I thought you would have told him. I didn't realise you were still expecting——'

'I wasn't,' Lara retorted. 'I guessed you preferred not to go on with the series, but Grant isn't always the easiest person to explain things to, and the day I chose to tell him was the day he had his heart attack.' She paused, then said, 'You don't have to go on with it, Lucas, just because he's tried to persuade you.'

'Because you don't want to go on with it?'

Lara shrugged. 'Our personal differences do seem to

make it difficult. I assumed that was why you let things drift.'

He looked at her long and hard. 'Yes, you're right, but personal differences needn't come into it. You have a job to do and I agreed to help you do it. I'm still willing to go on with it if you are.'

Lara was astonished. She had no alternative but to say yes. 'Well, what have you got for me this time?' she asked, keeping a smile in check, and trying not to listen to the rapid thumping of her heart. This time she would control her feelings for Lucas.

'A child, female, aged four, for a valve repair. She was admitted yesterday. We're going to operate in a few days. If you want to come along. . .'

'Of course I do. Thanks.' Lara was captured by his dark rather enigmatic gaze for a moment and, disconcerted, lowered her eyes. 'I do appreciate it, Lucas.'

'If you want you can get into Theatre gear and observe in Theatre,' he offered casually. 'You'll get a better view.'

Lara could hardly believe it. 'You mean that? You'll let me watch from the sidelines?' This was a totally unexpected dispensation.

'You are a doctor.' He was crazy, he told himself. This was no way to pay her back!

She glanced up at him. 'Do I take that as a compliment?'

He just looked at her without responding. After a longish pause he asked, 'How's the reading up on transplants going?'

'I've got a few questions. Are your wits clear enough now to answer them?'

'Try me.'

Lara did, fetching her notes and some of the papers she'd photocopied to the table. For an hour the talk was all professional. Lara made copious notes and was glad she understood the medical jargon.

Finally, picking up the bottle, Lucas said, 'Drink up your wine, Lara. Unless you want me to finish it off by myself and collapse in a stupor on your couch.'

'I could send down to the SCG for a couple of porters to remove you.'

'As I said, you're a hard woman, Dr Montague.'

Only not as hard as I ought to be, Lara thought. The wine was making her feel a little too relaxed. She was enjoying herself. It was almost like old times, sitting there with Lucas, sharing a giant pizza, talking about medicine, earnest sometimes, sharing a joke the next. Lucas had always been so companionable, so. . .human. Her awe of him had vanished on their first date, but never her admiration. She'd known even then that he was destined to be a top man in his profession. But success hadn't spoiled him. She smiled as the memories crowded back, of other occasions when Lucas had collapsed on her couch—not in this flat but the poky little one she'd had as a student—and ended up staying the night.

'What are you smiling at?'

'Nothing. Just thinking. . .'

'We had good times, didn't we?' Lucas murmured softly, reading her mind. 'Some of the best, Lara. . .'

Were her thoughts so transparent? Lara clamped her teeth on the inside of her bottom lip. As a wave of nostalgia engulfed her suddenly she wanted to cry. It was so stupid! Sitting here with Lucas, getting maudlin over the congealing remains of the pizza and the dregs of Italian wine. She glanced at him. Had he done this on purpose? Was he trying to undermine her? Was he hell-bent on proving that, despite everything, she still couldn't resist him physically? Was that to be her punishment?

Lara took a determined hold on herself. 'Yes, we did, Lucas. We had some wonderful times. But so do most people when they're young. There's no point in getting maudlin about it now.' She rose. 'I'll make the coffee.'

Lucas tipped the rest of the wine into his glass and followed her into the kitchen, carrying it. As she bent over the percolator he slid his fingers under her hair and caressed her nape, drawing the thick brown waves aside and putting his lips briefly to the pale skin beneath her ear.

Lara froze for an instant, electrified by the powerful sensation his touch caused to shaft right through her. She half turned, ready to scold, and found herself pinioned by his strong hard thighs against the kitchen bench. Lucas put the glass down and slid his hands lightly along her arms, brought her hands together within his greater grasp and raised them to his lips. No other man she'd ever known had kissed her hands. She'd asked him once why, teasing him for 'olde-worlde' gallantry, and he'd said, 'I like hands. They are capable of so many things. Creating, caring, giving pleasure. You have beautiful hands. I kiss them in homage!' She had laughed, but she'd liked it, and she still did. Lucas kissing each knuckle, each sensitive fingertip, was extra-ordinarily arousing. When his lips strayed to her palm, the sensations were even stronger, and she tried to pull her hands away. Guessing why, he smiled and let her go, but not to get away. He slid his arms around her, drawing her close and bending his head to her lips.

'Lucas. . .' Lara protested, but scarcely had breath for the name. His mouth claimed hers with a raw hunger, and for moments she was aware only of the taste of wine on both their lips, the warm masculine smell of him that reminded her faintly of clean things like soap and disinfectant, and the tantalising tang of hair and skin that was inexplicably sensual.

Lara's head was spinning from the wine and Lucas's own powerful ability to intoxicate. Her senses were reeling out of control, and her body seemed to have a will of its own, responding to his without shame. There was no way it was going to heed the small voice that protested inside her head. In a gesture of defeat she slipped her arms around Lucas's neck and gave a sigh of capitulation. It was wonderful not to fight, wonderful not to care, wonderful to want. . .and know you could have. . .

When the doorbell rang it was moments before it registered on either of them. A second pealing jerked them apart as though the caller could see.

'Who on earth. . .?' Lara ran her fingers through her ruffled hair and licked her lips, which felt swollen.

'Don't go!' Lucas put a restraining hand on her arm. 'They'll go away. They'll think you're not home.'

Lara was tempted, but the voice in her head she had been unable to heed before took command. Don't be an idiot, it said. Whoever's out there is your salvation. Part of her still didn't want to be saved, but in the end the rational part won.

'It's probably only my neighbour wanting me to collect her mail,' she said. 'She goes away quite often.'

As she spoke she moved quickly out of the kitchen and
into the hall, dreadfully conscious that her appearance
must be a complete giveaway. She prayed it was Alicia,
who never noticed anything personal about anyone else.
And as soon as she'd dealt with Alicia she would tell
Lucas it was time to go. And she would insist.

She opened the door and nearly gasped when she saw
Dirk Hoekstra standing there with a large folder in his
hands and swinging his motor-bike helmet.

'Hi,' he said.

'Oh, hi, Dirk.' Lara stared at him, mortified.

After a pause he said, 'All right if I come in?' He was
already in the hall, and Lara was weakly closing the
door. 'I've brought some proofs of those shots I took for
that piece you did on the rehabilitation of brain-dam-
aged victims of road trauma. I thought you'd like to see
them first. There are some good shots.'

'Thanks; that was thoughtful, Dirk,' Lara said. The
only way to handle the situation was matter-of-factly,
she decided. 'Come in. Would you like some coffee? I've
just made it. Lucas Turnbull is here. He came round to
tell me about an operation in a few days that I can go
and see. It's a bit of luck your coming tonight. You can
talk to him about the pictures for the series.' She could
see he wasn't convinced.

Dirk's expression was, in fact, suspicious, and even
more so when her visitor emerged from the kitchen
carrying a tray with cups and saucers and coffee-pot on
it. Lucas's face was guarded. No doubt he'd overheard
something of what she had been saying to Dirk.

'Dirk, this is Lucas Turnbull.' Lara managed to sound
a little less embarrassed. 'Lucas, this is *New Era*'s chief
photographer. He's brought some pics for me to look at.'

Lucas set the tray on the table. 'I'll get another cup.' He went out.

Dirk said in a low sarcastic tone, 'If I'm interrupting anything. . .'

Lara, with diffculty, replied, 'Only a barrage of questions. I take every opportunity I can to pick Lucas's brains. Sit down. I'll just get some biscuits to have with coffee.'

She met Lucas in the kitchen doorway. 'Get rid of him,' he muttered.

'No!' Her eyes were stormy as they met his defiantly.

'You were expecting him,' he accused.

'I wasn't.'

Lara knew he didn't believe her. Well, it didn't matter what either of them thought about the other, or her. The sooner they both went the better she would like it. And somehow she was going to have to make sure they went together. She didn't want to be left alone with either.

CHAPTER SIX

LARA went to the hospital the day before the scheduled operation. Lucas had told her that the parents of the four-year-old were agreeable to being interviewed and photographed.

'The kid's thrilled about having her photo in the paper,' he said drily when he phoned to let Lara know the situation. 'I hope you won't over-excite her.'

'I'll try not to,' Lara promised. Their conversation was brief and he made no reference to the night at her place when Dirk had arrived at a timely, or untimely, moment, depending on the point of view.

She bought a picture book for the small patient and wrapped it in colourful paper, attaching a jolly get-well card, and she and Dirk went together to the ward where Jessica Price was. Her parents were with her as arranged. They introduced themselves as Karen and Ross.

Lara shook hands with them, noting that their outward normality concealed understandable anxiety. 'It's good of you to let me feature Jessica's operation,' she said. 'Many people would regard it as an invasion of privacy.'

Karen nodded. 'We thought about it very carefully first, and we decided that it's important for people to read about the kind of problems they might have in their own families, with their children.' She added brightly,

'We always read your articles. They're so down to earth and informative.'

'Reassuring,' put in her husband.

Lara smiled. 'I try to be.'

Karen said impulsively, 'We trust you. . .' She broke off, embarrassed. 'I mean, we know you'll write a good article. . .'

Lara was touched. 'Thank you.' She turned to the child in the bed. Jessica was small for her age, not unusual for a child with patent ductus arteriosus. Her fine fair hair clung about her heart-shaped face in soft curls and her blue eyes were full of curiosity and a little anxiety. She was going to make a very appealing picture.

'Hello, Jessica,' Lara said. 'I thought you might be getting a bit bored in here so I brought you something to read.' She handed over the book, which the child politely thanked her for and eagerly unwrapped. She looked up with pleasure at her parents.

'I haven't got this one!'

'She loves books,' Ross confided. 'That was a nice thought, Dr Montague.'

For half an hour she talked to the little girl's parents about how and when their daughter's condition had been diagnosed, and about their other children, while Dirk took some photographs and Jessica read her new book. Nurses came and went breezily, and just as Lara was about to leave Lucas arrived.

Lara had spoken to him on the phone, but had not seen him since the night he had brought the pizza to her place and Dirk had turned up. The night she had let her emotions get rather too much out of control. The sight of him gave her the kind of jolt she was having to become accustomed to. She might regret the fact, but the truth was that Lucas had lost none of his attraction for her. He was wearing a white coat today and for some reason that made him look even more compelling than in an ordinary suit.

'How's it going?' he asked cheerfully, and chatted with all his considerable charm to the Prices, parents and daughter.

Lara was amused but unsurprised to discover that he was a definite hit with all three. He quite clearly had the complete confidence of Karen and Ross, and Jessica fluttered her eyelashes at him beguilingly.

Lucas donned his stethoscope and sat on the edge of the bed. 'Now, young lady, let's have a listen to that murmur. I wonder what it's saying today. "Going to get better, going to get better. . ."'

'The man took photos,' Jessica informed him, pointing at Dirk. 'I'm going to have my picture in the paper.' She pouted proudly.

'Terrific. You'll be famous,' said Lucas. He looked over his shoulder at Lara. 'Want to listen?'

Lara hesitated, then took the proffered stethoscope and bent over the child. It was an odd feeling to do even so small a medical task after such a long time. She felt strangely nervous. She listened to the distinct systolic murmur for a moment, then smiled at Jessica, who said, 'I've got too many noises in there, so I have to get rid of one.'

Lara smiled up at Lucas as she unhooked the stethoscope arms from her ears. 'That's one way of putting it, I guess!'

'You may quote me,' he said in a dry tone. Then he spoke to the child again. 'Have you been doing your breathing exercises the way the physiotherapist told you?'

Jessica nodded. Her blue eyes were impish. 'Teddy has too! He's got a murmur just like me.'

'Let me listen.' Lucas applied the stethoscope to the toy bear's chest, frowning. 'What do you think, Dr Montague?'

Lara played the game. 'Amazing! Just like Jessica's.'

Lucas tapped both bear and patient on the nose. 'OK,' he said briskly. 'We'll fix both of you!'

Dirk leaned over Lara's shoulder. 'I've got to go, Caro. Got another assignment.'

He would continue calling her Caro, she thought, and, once she had finished with the SCG and Lucas Turnbull, she would be Caroline to everyone else again. 'Sure,' she said. 'Take care.' She saw Lucas glance at the photographer with something like disdain, and was reminded that Dirk had successfully frustrated him that night at her place. She had managed to get rid of both of them together by pleading tiredness, and, since neither had seemed inclined to leave before the other, the only thing they could agree on was leaving together.

Dirk had said the next day, 'Is there something between you and the high-flying surgeon?' And she had answered, 'No. I just happen to know him from way back.' There was no point in confessing that she had been engaged to Lucas. Dirk had looked sceptical, and Lara didn't doubt that Lucas probably felt the same about the photographer. As a result of denying any involvement with Lucas, Lara had found herself agreeing to a date with Dirk. They'd had dinner and gone to a nightclub, and she'd enjoyed herself well enough. Dirk had seemed content with a goodnight kiss, to her relief, and later she'd told herself that she was a lot safer with him, and maybe it would be a good thing to let Lucas think there was more to her relationship with Dirk than there actually was.

When Lara left the ward, Lucas walked with her and offered her a cup of coffee in his office.

'I'll give you a run-down on the Price child's history and prognosis,' he said generously.

'Thanks.' She could hardly refuse the invitation in the face of that offer.

Ensconced in a well-padded armchair in his office, she watched him pour two cups of coffee from the jug keeping hot on the filter machine's hotplate.

'Decaffeinated,' he said, handing her a fine-bone cup and saucer with the hospital insignia on it.

'You're not into herb tea yet?' Lara chided.

Lucas pulled a face. 'Too diuretic!' And Lara laughed.

Instead of taking the chair behind it, he perched on the edge of the desk, rather too close for Lara's comfort.

'Tell me about Jessica,' she said. 'Her parents said she was diagnosed when they took her to the doctor with a bout of bronchitis.'

'That's right.' He looked at her keenly. 'You're aware of the anatomical indications of patent ductus arteriosus?'

Lara bridled slightly. 'Of course! My memory isn't that stultified,' she retorted.

'Tell me.'

'I'm not a raw student, Lucas!' she said, resenting the quiz.

'It doesn't hurt to get the facts right,' he responded evenly. 'Let's see how much you do remember.'

Lara lifted her chin. 'For your information, Mr

Turnbull, the ductus arteriosus is a natural opening from the aorta to the pulmonary artery which is necessary to the foetus but which usually closes up after birth, but sometimes doesn't. Oxygenated blood from the aorta being pumped into the pulmonary artery causes increased cardiac output and the symptoms commonly known as a murmur. For some unknown reason girls are twice as likely to be affected as boys.'

'Treatment?' demanded her inquisitor.

'Ligation of the ductus arteriosus as soon after diagnosis as possible, through a left thoracotomy.'

Lucas smiled. 'Not bad for a rusty operator.'

'Thank *you*!'

'I'm glad to see you haven't forgotten your medical terminology,' Lucas said rather drily. 'Now tell me—how would you describe it to the patient's parents, or. . .' his mouth twitched in a half-smile '. . .to your avid readers?'

'You think I just recited that parrot-fashion?' Lara said, mildly outraged.

He just smiled and waited. Needled, she said briskly, with a touch of acid, 'I would explain, of course, that a ductus arteriosus is a passage connecting the artery that serves the lungs and the aorta, which is the artery that supplies blood to all the body. It is only necessary to circulation of blood while the baby is growing and usually, as I said, closes after birth. When it doesn't the hole may need to be closed surgically through an incision in the left side of the patient's thorax, or chest.'

Lucas nodded. 'Explaining procedures to patients in lay terms is a skill many physicians and surgeons lack.' His eyes were intently on her face. 'Your talents are wasted on a popular newspaper.'

'That's a matter of opinion,' Lara said stiffly.

Lucas did not comment further, but he was apparently still determined to quiz her. He rapped out, 'Do you remember what Fallot's tetrology is?'

Lara's recent reading had helped her memory so she was able to say, 'Yes. It's another congenital condition, a combination of four defects: pulmonary stenosis, hypertrophy of the right ventricle, ventricular septal defect and an overriding aorta. Cyanosis is usually obvious in the patient, especially when exercising. Convulsions may occur. Surgery recommended to correct the malformations. Will that do?' She sighed, 'No, I suppose you want it in lay terms too?'

'Just to be sure you do know what you're talking about.'

He knows I do, she thought in annoyance, but he's enjoying putting me through this for some reason. Gritting her teeth for a moment, she then said, 'Some babies are born with several defects to the heart's and lungs' vascular system, such as narrowing of an artery, thickening of the wall of the right ventricle, and other malformations which can all usually be corrected by surgery. I think any further explanation might become boring, but I'll try to use diagrams where I can.'

'An excellent idea. We'll be doing a Fallot's tetrology later this week, and in fact we'll also be correcting a coarctation of the aorta and an atrial septal defect. . .'

'For coarctation read narrowing,' intoned Lara, 'and for atrial septal defect let's just say "hole" again, shall we?' She added stiffly, 'I don't blind my readers with medical jargon, Lucas, but neither do I underestimate their intelligence.' She laughed lightly. 'They watch a lot of television, you know!'

He acknowledged her remark with a curt nod. 'I think you should be able to glean enough material for a fairly comprehensive piece on congenital heart disease in young children. That is bound to appeal, I would imagine.'

'Definitely.' Before he could come up with any more medical quizzes, she asked, 'Any transplant candidates in the offing?'

'Two,' Lucas told her. 'Adults. But the problem, as you know, is finding donors. We have an Australia-wide alert network so we can send a recovery team off at a moment's notice, but available doesn't always mean suitable.'

'I don't think I'd like someone else's heart. . .' Lara mused slowly.

'That's just emotional. If you were dying I reckon you would,' said Lucas. He eyed her steadily. 'More important is the long-term effect on society, whether transplants are ethical and economical. Should we spend large sums of money extending the life-spans of a few or on alleviating the suffering of many?'

Lara was surprised at this view from Lucas. 'You have doubts?'

'The path of medicine is strewn with doubts,' he said, 'and that, I suppose, is as it should be. We should never be too complacent, not about science, or about ethics.'

Lara nodded agreement. 'Any more questions, Mr Turnbull, or have I passed the oral?' she enquired archly.

'You pass.' In more ways than one, he thought, letting his gaze drift idly down over her—to him, and he didn't doubt plenty of other men—very desirable form. Her skirt had ridden up over her crossed knees, showing an expanse of smooth thigh and shapely calves. The green corduroy suit enhanced her sleek brown hair and velvety eyes. She still had beautiful hands too, with longish fingers and neatly trimmed nails unadorned by varnish. He wanted to touch. . .but after the night he'd almost made love to her he wasn't so sure he should continue along that line, even if she was as willing as she'd seemed then. This other guy, the photographer, was in the way for a start. How intimate were they? he wondered jealously. Well, Dirk whatever-his-name-was would learn in due course, no doubt, that Lara was unlikely to become a permanent part of his life. Or did the man have the power to change her mind? Lucas felt uncomfortable with that thought.

'It's time I was going,' Lara said as she handed him her empty cup. 'Thanks for the coffee.'

'You're welcome.' He straightened up as she rose, and they were close for a moment. A whiff of her perfume swirled around him. She still used the same inexpensive, unsophisticated fresh-flowers scent. He used to buy her bottles of it. . .and she'd always pretended to be so thrilled, so appreciative that he'd noticed her current bottle was running low. Pretended? No, she'd been genuine. That was one of the things he'd liked about her—her appreciation of what others did for her and her own generous and unselfish nature. It was one of the reasons he'd fallen in love with her. Too soon, he reflected now. When she was nineteen the age difference had seemed too great for her. But now—now it was irrelevant. And, to his chagrin, he wanted her more than ever.

'We'll see you tomorrow, then,' he said, pushing the past resolutely back where it belonged. 'Don't be late.'

'Hardly!'

He did not walk to the lifts with her today. He was obviously busy and she had taken up too much of his time already. Lara rode all the way to the ground floor before she realised she had left her umbrella in his office. The forecast had been showers later, but as she reached the foyer she could see through the glass-walled entrance that it was raining already. With an exclamation of annoyance she rode back up to Lucas's floor again and hurried along the corridor to his office, bypassing the reception area.

His door was half open and she was about to give a perfunctory knock and push it wider when she realised that Lucas had another visitor. Sister Ioannidis. The theatre nurse was sitting on the front edge of the desk, her legs crossed so that her uniform had ridden up to display very shapely thighs and trim ankles. Lucas was standing beside her and some remark he made, which Lara did not catch, made Teresa give a ripple of laughter. And then Lucas's hand was on her thigh and he was bending forward. Lara drew in a sharp breath, but they were too absorbed in the kiss to notice that they were observed. Lara hurried away, unaccountably shaken by what she had seen. If she'd needed any confirmation that Lucas and Teresa were on intimate terms she had it now. So what? she said to herself. It doesn't make an atom of difference to me.

In the foyer she gazed bleakly at the rain, now pelting down. She was about to ask Reception to call her a taxi when Josh Edwards strode across to her.

'Caroline—Lara, my dear,' he said jovially. 'I don't know what to call you now!'

'I answer to both,' she said.

'What a day!' he exclaimed. 'Bright sunshine this morning, now a storm.' He considered her lack of raincoat or umbrella. 'You've got your car?'

'No, not today. It's in for a service. I came on the tram.'

'No brolly?'

'I left it in Lucas's office,' she said. 'I was——'

'No need,' he said. 'I'll send someone up for you.' He crossed to the reception desk and a moment later one of the junior receptionists went scurrying towards the lifts.

'Thanks,' Lara said, relieved, and couldn't help thinking that it would serve Lucas right if the girl caught him in a compromising position, which, she agreed with herself, was not at all charitable. Why should she gloat over his pleasure being curtailed?

Josh chatted to her until the girl arrived back with her umbrella. If she had seen anything worth gossiping about she gave no sign of it.

'Lucas being co-operative?' Josh was saying.

'Very. I'm to see three ops this week, all of them congenital heart disease involving children. It'll be a good angle. He actually invited me to go into the theatre to watch.'

Josh lifted a surprised eyebrow. 'You must have a way with you, my dear.' As he spoke the paging system called for him and, with a hasty goodbye, he left her.

Lara decided to forget the taxi as the rain was easing off. She was lucky, as a tram going to the city came along almost immediately, and she climbed aboard only slightly damp.

As she slumped into a seat the woman next to her glanced at her, then looked again and said tentatively, 'Lara?'

Lara turned to face her and her eyes widened. 'Mrs Turnbull! Goodness, what a coincidence.' She looked at the older woman uncertainly.

'It is you,' the rather frail elderly lady said. 'I thought it was. Lucas told me he'd seen you and what you were doing.'

Lara looked for reproach, but found none. She was relieved to find that, after all, Lucas's mother apparently bore her no grudge. 'Yes, it was quite a surprise to run into him at South City General. I thought he was in America.' And then she remembered why he was not. 'I'm so sorry about your husband.'

Vera Turnbull's eyes filled with tears and she turned quickly to look out of the window, then, getting a grip on herself, said in a firm voice. 'It was a terrible blow, Lara. I didn't realise. . .how much I would miss him. . .' Her voice wavered a little. 'I don't know what I would have done if Lucas hadn't come back. He's been so wonderful. . .'

'It was lucky the position at SCG came up,' Lara said.

'Yes. I felt so badly about him giving up his job in the States just for me, but he insisted on coming home.' She gave a small sigh. 'I am lucky to have such a considerate son.' Her moment of grief had passed, and in a more normal tone she asked, 'And what about you, my dear? You're happy in your work? Did Lucas tell you I always read your articles? So you're Caroline Kelly—I never would have guessed!'

'Yes, I enjoy my work very much,' Lara said.

'You don't ever think about going back to medicine?'

'No.'

'Don't you ever yearn to be doing it instead of reporting it?' Mrs Turnbull had always been incisive.

Like her son. 'It's probably rude of me to say so, and I don't mean any denigration of your present profession, but it seems such a waste. . .'

'Oh, I get little urges now and then to put on a white coat and a stethoscope,' Lara heard herself admitting. 'But I don't see myself ever going back to it now.'

'That's a pity. You were so dedicated once.' Vera Turnbull's eyes were dark like her son's, and as penetrating. Then she smiled and patted Lara's arm as though in apology for unspoken words. 'You must come and have dinner with us soon,' she said. 'I told Lucas to ask you. He thinks I'm not up to entertaining, but I want to. I mustn't brood. That's why I'm going into town today on my own. I've been holing myself up in that old house for too long already, afraid to go out because I might break down.'

'It doesn't matter if you do,' Lara said quietly. 'Nobody will mind.'

Mrs Turnbull bit her lip and half smiled. 'You're right, of course. And I know it. So here I am, trotting off to the city to go window shopping. I might even buy myself a new dress. Whenever I was a bit down Philip always used to say, "Vera, go and buy yourself something nice to wear. Cheer yourself up."'

Lara laughed. 'It used to be "go buy yourself a new hat", didn't it? But hats seem to have gone out of fashion.'

'With all this talk about skin cancer and the ozone layer they'll be back in fashion before long, I suppose,' said Mrs Turnbull. 'I don't see people heeding the warnings, though, do you?' She chuckled. 'You're a doctor—do *you* wear a hat?'

'No. Not ordinarily, I must confess, but in summer, if

I'm going to be out in the sun for a long stretch, I do try to remember and I use a sun-screen.'

'I've had two skin cancers removed,' Mrs Turnbull told her, pointing to the now invisible sites on her face. 'And I hope I don't develop any more. But when I was young I loved the beach. We never dreamed there was any danger in getting suntanned and never thought anything of it.'

The tram was clanking along Spencer Street and Lara reached up and pulled the cord. 'I get off here,' she said. 'My office is in Lonsdale Street.'

'I'm so glad we met,' said Vera warmly. 'You've cheered me enormously. You will come to dinner soon, won't you, Lara? Shall we say Friday next week? Will you be free?'

The tram was slowing at the stop. Lara didn't have the heart to say no when Vera looked so eager. 'Yes, all right,' she said. 'I'd love to.'

'Lucas will bring you,' his mother said as Lara alighted from the tram.

No, he won't, Lara said firmly to herself. I'll drive myself.

Lara arrived at the hospital next day with plenty of time to spare so that she could see Jessica and her parents beforehand.

The Prices were naturally in a state of some anxiety, but putting a brave face on it. They looked pleased to see Lara and she did her best to add extra reassurance.

'It's quite a common operation, and you've got one of the best surgeons in Australia looking after her. A great team, in fact.'

Trying to laugh and sounding nervous, Karen Price said, 'We're terrible worriers!'

'Most parents are. That's natural.' Lara added, 'Has Mr Turnbull been up yet?'

As she spoke Lucas arrived. Lara drew back after he had greeted the Prices and her. He was genial but not too hearty, and exuded confidence. He chatted easily to Jessica, explaining what was going to happen, how a man called an anaesthetist was going to prick her skin with a needle and she was going to go to sleep for a while.

'Like Sleeping Beauty,' said Jessica, who seemed not in the least concerned about the 'adventure'.

Lucas smiled. 'Exactly. And when you wake up that little hole in your heart will have been mended and you won't have felt a thing.'

'It's like magic,' said Jessica.

Lucas glanced at Lara and they exchanged a smile. Lucas ruffled the child's fair hair. 'You're a brave girl, Jessica.'

'What about Teddy?' the child asked. She was clutching the bear tightly and he was obviously her favourite toy.

'His turn after you,' said Lucas. 'He can go along with you to see what happens.'

'Oh, goody,' said Jessica. 'Then he won't be frightened.'

Lucas dug his hand in his pocket. 'I've brought something specially for Teddy, so he won't spread any germs around.'

Lara was amused and touched to see him unfold a gauze mask and with all seriousness fasten it over the toy bear's snout. Jessica was delighted. She giggled and fluttered her long lashes at Lucas.

Lucas spent a few more minutes with the child and her parents, then he and Lara went together to the theatre suite.

'You bumped into my mother yesterday,' he remarked.

'Yes, wasn't that a coincidence? I sat down next to her on the tram without realising at first.'

'It's been a long time,' Lucas said, 'and Dad's death has aged her.'

'She was a little tearful at first, but she seemed to cheer up a bit as we chatted. Did she have a good day in town?'

'Yes. She said seeing you helped a lot. I don't know what you said to her, but it seemed to make an impression. She said you were a loss to the medical profession.'

'And you never lose an opportunity to remind me!' Lara retorted sharply.

Lucas ignored the response. 'You're coming to dinner next Friday, I gather.'

'I could hardly say no.'

'Did you want to?'

Lara lifted her eyes and met a steady gaze. She wished she knew what she did want. Maybe she *was* fickle and contrary and grasshopper-minded, as she was sure Lucas believed. 'The situation is a little awkward,' she said. 'Don't you think so?'

'Not at all.' He gave her a slightly twisted smile as they walked into the coffee-room. 'Unless you're suffering from a guilty conscience.'

Lara was fortunately not required to answer that

rather barbed remark as they were no longer alone. There were several people in the coffee-room, including Graham Butterworth. He monopolised her immediately that someone else buttonholed Lucas.

'So Lucas is allowing you to invade the hallowed precinct of his theatre today,' he said.

'I'm honoured.'

He grinned. 'Watch it! He'll have you assisting before you know where you are.'

'I think that might be against the rules,' Lara pointed out.

Graham pulled a face. 'The only rules Lucas adheres to are his own!'

Lucas returned to interrupt their conversation with the brusque reminder that there was work to be done. 'They're bringing Jessica down shortly,' he said to Lara. 'If you want to see her in Reception I suggest you go along there now.'

Lara did so. The little girl was still bright as a button, despite her pre-med, and now only her mother was with her. Karen's smile belied her nervousness. She said, 'I'll be glad when this is over. It's the first time any of my children has had to have surgery or has even been in hospital.'

'Jessica's very brave,' said Lara.

'She is, isn't she? Much braver than I am! She sees it as a big adventure—thanks to Mr Turnbull. He's so good with children. I suppose he's married with kiddies of his own.'

'No, he isn't,' Lara told her, and wondered just how long that state might endure. If Teresa had her way perhaps not long at all. Lucas would make a good father, she agreed, and then left mother and daughter to go and change into a theatre gown. Although she was not going to come into contact with the patient, she was still required to wear a gown and cap and mask.

As she went through the procedure Lara felt even stranger than she had on the previous occasion she had watched an operation because today she was going to be closer to the action, and, memory being what it was, it was hard not to feel that she was in fact part of that action.

'It's easy to see you're a doctor,' the nurse who helped her into her sterile gown and cap said. 'You sort of do things automatically.'

'I must have been thoroughly trained, I suppose,' Lara said.

'Where was that?' the girl asked interestedly.

'Sydney. The Southern Cross.'

'My brother's there. He's older than me. He's a cardiologist. He's been there for years. Maybe you know him. Brett Gordon?'

Lara shook her head. 'No, sorry, I don't recall the name. . .so many. . .'

'Sure. But funnier coincidences have happened. Maybe he'll remember you. I'll ask him.'

'I doubt it. An awful lot of med students and interns pass through large teaching hospitals.'

'Right, there you go,' said the nurse, tying the last tape. 'Have a good day!'

Lara looked around for Lucas but he had abandoned her. Since she knew where to go and what to do, and did not want to be a bother to anyone, she made her way into the theatre being used for Jessica's operation. As she entered she felt an involuntary surge of adrenalin, even though she was not participating. The sights and sounds and smells brought memories rushing back, and she felt the little thrill of power tempered by the tiny apprehension that had always accompanied her in the theatre.

There was only one thing to spoil it for her today and that was discovering that Teresa was scrubbing for Lucas.

'Hello, Teresa,' Lara said pleasantly as she almost bumped into her.

Dark Greek eyes met hers with a hostile expression. 'Oh, hi,' the girl said diffidently. She added, 'You'd better sit over there,' and indicated a stool against a far wall.

'Thanks.' Lara obeyed, as she wanted to be as unobtrusive as possible, but the positioning of the stool meant that her view of proceedings would be limited. She was likely to see nothing but green-gowned backs. She had a strong suspicion that Teresa had done this on purpose.

When Graham, the anaesthetist, came in, he stopped for a brief word. 'You won't be able to see much from there,' he said. 'Come closer to the table.'

'I don't want to be pushy,' Lara said doubtfully. It just might have been Lucas who had positioned the stool, and she didn't want to take liberties.

'I'll speak to Lucas,' Graham insisted.

A few minutes later the nurse who was the team's 'runner' came over and told Lara she could move up closer if she wanted to and to stand wherever she could best see what was happening. 'So long as you don't impede anyone,' she said.

'Did Mr Turnbull say so?' Lara asked.

The nurse nodded.

Suddenly the purposeful bustling quietened, and the

operation began. Lara watched, fascinated as she always had been by delicate surgical procedures. Her eyes shifted back and forth from Lucas's hands to his face as he worked, his assistant opposite him, Teresa beside him.

She was very efficient, Lara noted as instruments passed from her to Lucas with barely a word spoken, and she never missed her cue, always handing him the exact instrument he required, never fumbling, her concentration as steady as his.

She noted too the glances, from him to her and the way Teresa's eyes watched his face more than his hands. Possessively, Lara thought. Lovingly. The girl was in love with Lucas, she felt certain. There was something intuitive in this knowledge, how just by looking at the nurse she could, from the tiniest of movements, deduce her feelings. It wasn't until near the end of the operation that she became aware suddenly and shockingly of the reason for her remarkable insight. She knew Teresa was in love with Lucas because she was in love with him herself.

The realisation was heart-stopping. She knew now why she had never been able to fall in love with anyone else. Lucas Turnbull still owned her heart. True, she had jilted him, but she hadn't stopped loving him. She had been afraid marriage might mean giving up her career, so she had given up Lucas, but her heart had never let go of him completely. It had all been too soon ten years ago. Now it was all too late.

'I'm too young,' she had told Lucas in the letter cancelling their wedding. 'I can't go through with it. . . If we'd met in ten years' time. . .'

It was ten years later now, but too late. By jilting him

she had forfeited his trust and his respect. He was still attracted to her, she knew that, and he would make love to her if she would let him, but he wouldn't chance his pride again. He would never ask her for a commitment now: hadn't he said so? Bleakly, she choked on the surge of emotion, wanting to burst through the swing doors and run. But she couldn't—not yet, not tonight, not even tomorrow. The ordeal must be endured until she'd completed her heart-surgery series. After that she would never see him again. Teresa had no need to be jealous. No need at all.

CHAPTER SEVEN

AT THE end of the operation Lara felt drained, not from the effort of concentrating on the delicate surgical repair to a little girl's heart, but from trying to keep control of her emotions. If only this were the end of the whole project, she thought, and she didn't have to endure more. If only the new cardiac surgery department director had been anyone but Lucas Turnbull. If only she weren't still in love with him. . .

Afterwards, seeing that he was in consultation with the surgeon who had assisted him, Lara thought she would be able to escape without speaking to him, but she was wrong. She went through to the recovery-room, where she knew Karen Price would be allowed to sit with her daughter until the child recovered consciousness, and found Lucas right behind her as she went in.

Unable to help herself, Lara looked back into his face, framed still by the ridiculous green cap, and saw the tension of concentration still lingering there.

'Did you have a good enough view?' he enquired.

'Yes, thanks.' She paused. 'It all went very well.'

'Yes. She's a healthy child. She'll be right as rain.'

Karen Price looked up in surprise and delight when Lucas and Lara entered. The recovery-room sister frowned at the invasion, but Lucas threw her a cheery greeting and a brief explanation for Lara's presence, and the woman melted into smiles.

Lucas also beamed at Karen Price. 'Jessie'll come

round shortly,' he said. He inspected the IV and chest drain and checked the oxygen mask. 'And then she'll be moved to an intensive-care ward. Are you staying over tonight, Karen?' He sounded as kindly as a near relative, or as though he'd known Karen Price and her family for years.

'Yes, I am,' Jessica's mother said. She looked less tense now, but there was still anxiety in her face.

He clasped her hand. 'Good. Stay with her until she comes round and until she goes to sleep naturally, then she won't feel strange. You'll have a nurse specialling her for the first twenty-four hours, which is normal procedure.'

'She's going to be all right, isn't she?' Karen asked the question at last.

Lucas patted her shoulder. 'Of course. There were no problems. It was a very straightforward procedure. She'll be up and about playing before you know it.' His smile reinforced the reassuring words.

'Thank you,' Karen said with a heartfelt sigh, and tears started in her eyes. 'Thank you so much, Doctor. . .'

'I'd better go and change,' Lara said, indicating her theatre garb as they left the recovery-room, Lucas with her, giving her snippets of information, which she knew she would later be hard put to remember. She couldn't seem to concentrate on anything except the sound of his voice.

As one of the nurses was about to untie her gown he intervened.

'I'll do that,' he said, peremptorily dismissing the girl, who gave Lara an envious glance.

'What's this—VIP treatment?' Lara said lightly, hoping her shattered composure was well concealed.

He pulled the back ties undone, and even so light a touch set her nerves aflame. Lara stepped away.

'Now undo me, please,' he said, turning his back.

Over his shoulder Lara saw Teresa hurrying towards him, then stopping in her tracks as she saw that her help was not required. Apparently unaware of the nurse's stricken expression, Lucas called her over and exchanged a few words about something that hadn't been quite as he'd wanted it. Lara wished he hadn't chosen to criticise the nurse in front of her. Teresa clearly did not appreciate it. She stalked off huffily.

Lucas turned back to Lara and placed a hand on her shoulder. 'Off home now?'

'Yes.'

'You have your car?'

'No, it's being serviced. I couldn't get it back today because they've had staff off with flu and a run of urgent repairs. I came by tram.'

'I'll run you home.'

'No, really, Lucas,' Lara protested. 'I know you must be busy.'

'I'm off now myself as it happens,' he said.

'Was Jessica your only op today?' Lara queried.

'Yes. Meet me in the foyer in ten minutes.'

Having changed back into her clothes and shoes, Lara went down to the entrance. Lucas was not there and he didn't arrive for another ten minutes. She gazed at the mural, trying to keep her mind distracted. She really should have refused his offer of a lift. She ought to go now. She could pretend later that she'd thought he must have been delayed. But she left the decision too long. Lucas appeared and was apologetic.

'Sorry I kept you. A small problem. . .'

'Jessica?' queried Lara anxiously.

'No. An administrative matter!' He grimaced, then looked intently at her. 'I was afraid you might have left.'

'I was just thinking about it.'

'I'm glad you didn't.' He smiled briefly. 'You must be as hungry as I am, so we'll eat somewhere on the way.' He frowned at the reluctance in her eyes. 'Too early for you?'

'No. . .' She felt she couldn't eat a thing, but saying no to Lucas was always harder than she imagined.

He drove to a small Greek restaurant he told her he had recently discovered, and Lara guessed who had facilitated that discovery.

'I suppose Teresa recommended it,' she commented as they entered.

'Mmm. As a matter of fact her father and brother own it.'

Lara had not expected that. She was a little surprised that Lucas had brought her here. Teresa was bound to get to know if Lucas was known to the family, as he must be if Teresa had brought him here. Was he insensitive or just anxious to let Teresa find out that he took other women out? Lara surprised herself by feeling almost sorry for the other woman. But acknowledging that Lucas was—probably always had been—a philanderer didn't alter her feelings for him one iota.

'Hello, George,' Lucas greeted the white-aproned waiter cheerfully.

'Hello, Mr Turnbull. You're early. We only just opened.'

'We're starving,' Lucas said as they were shown to a table in the almost deserted restaurant. 'And, as we're going to a show later, we need to eat early.'

'Teresa's brother,' Lucas explained as George went to fetch the menus. He ignored the astonished look on Lara's face, her sharp intake of breath.

Lara said, 'Why did you tell him we're going to a show when we aren't?'

He smiled across the table at her. 'Yes, we are. I was given two tickets to *Phantom of the Opera* today, and I bet you haven't seen it yet.'

His calm assumption that she would not object took Lara's breath away. 'Why don't you take your mother?' she suggested, dismayed at the thought of spending the whole evening with him while her emotions were in such a high old state of turmoil.

'She's already going next week with some friends. She's beginning to come out of her shell, I'm glad to say, and when one of her old cronies rang to ask if she wanted to join the theatre party again—there are a dozen of them and they've been subscribers to the Melbourne Theatre Company seasons for years—she decided she would.'

Blankly, Lara stared at the menu George put in front of her. She could say no. She could insist she wanted to write up her article while it was still fresh in her mind. But she knew she hadn't the will-power to do that. She was going to go out tonight with Lucas because, even though loving him was painful, she couldn't resist an opportunity to be with him. There would be so few such opportunities, she told herself, that it would be foolish not to make the most of them. Even if it did mean heartbreak later.

'If we hurry up there'll be time for us both to go home
and change,' Lucas said, glancing at the time. 'I'll pick
you up again about seven-thirty.'

Lara made a feeble protest. 'What about my article?'

'You can get up early tomorrow and do it,' Lucas
suggested blithely. 'You'll be fresher then.'

In spite of herself, Lara smiled. 'You always were a
master of the *fait accompli*, weren't you, Lucas?'

His face was sombre and there was no hint of humour
in his eyes when he said, 'Was I? I failed to get you to
the altar, as I recall.'

'Maybe that was fate putting a curb on your
impulsiveness.'

'Huh! Probably,' he conceded. And surely, he thought,
he had more sense than to try and rectify his earlier
failure now? He must stop seeing her as a challenge to
be met and conquered. He'd come to terms with her
rejection long ago. Besides, she'd made it very clear that
marriage was still not on her agenda. Unless that was
just for his benefit—the thought of the photographer
still bugged him.

George hurried up their orders and they ate with one
eye on the clock. Lara, who had not been hungry,
regained her appetite somewhat when her stuffed auber-
gine arrived, and the delicious dessert of figs was no
problem either. Her mood changed and she felt quite
light-hearted when they left, forgetting for the moment
that she was trespassing on Teresa's territory. Instead
she pretended to herself that it was just as it used to be,
going out with the man she loved and was going to
marry. . . She even caught herself idly massaging the
third finger of her left hand where a diamond and
sapphire ring had once fitted so snugly.

The foolishness of her fantasy overcame her several times while she was showering and changing, but she knew of no way to put Lucas off now. And deep down she didn't want to. It was a clear case of letting her heart rule her head, she thought glumly.

Dressed in a charcoal-grey two-piece suit with snowy white fichu, long narrow sleeves and a slim skirt, she surveyed her reflection in the long mirror on the door of the wardrobe critically. She was slimmer than she had been ten years ago, and her features had settled into a maturity that even she could see. The child had long since turned into a woman.

'Why didn't I marry him?' she whispered. 'How could I have been such a fool?'

She sank down miserably on the dressing-table stool to make up her face. With a clear skin with a good colour, naturally well-shaped eyebrows and thick lashes, she needed little to enhance her appearance and was content with a touch of mascara and a deep-red lipstick. She sprayed a little perfume on her wrists and slipped her black-stockinged feet into high-heeled pumps. As she dropped cosmetics, comb, handkerchief and wallet into a black-beaded bag, her eye was arrested by the date on the desk calendar she kept on her dressing-table and on which she jotted reminders. She stared at it for a moment as its significance slowly sank in.

'Oh, no!' she breathed. And then, in a kind of panic, 'Does he remember?'

It was the date on which they should have been married. May the twenty-third. For years it had been engraved on her mind, a guilty reminder each year of what she had done, but for the last few years she had managed to forget, to forgive herself. But now it seemed to accuse her all over again.

Her mouth tilted wryly. If they had married tonight's outing would have been their tenth-anniversary celebration. Now the date only added a terrible poignancy to being with Lucas. She hoped he didn't remember.

Imagine having been married for ten years to Lucas! Lara thought wistfully as she waited for him to call for her. What a fool she had been to throw it all away because she was afraid her career would suffer, because she had let her family convince her that he was too old for her, and more importantly that she was too young to get married.

The pressures at home had been strong. Ever since her father had married again Lara had felt left out of her new family. Marjorie had two daughters a few years older than Lara who were academically brilliant. Right from the start Lara had felt very much in their shadow. So, besides wanting to be a doctor more than anything else herself, she had also been desperately keen to please her father so that he wouldn't feel ashamed of her.

Her stepsisters were headed for careers in architecture and the law. Medicine compared very favourably. They were also ardent feminists who scorned marriage, and they'd made dire predictions about Lara's future if she married so young, especially someone with ambitions of his own. Lucas had never made any secret of the fact that he was aiming high, that a consultancy was his first goal, and, after that, who knew? 'You'd be overshadowed completely,' they'd told Lara. Her father, too, had begged her not to risk wasting her education. As he'd still been helping her financially Lara had felt she had a debt to repay by being at least as successful as her stepsisters. Weighed down by pressures at home and her own misgivings about being able to cope with marriage and a career, afraid she would always be trailing in the wake of Lucas, or obliged to make sacrifices in her own career to suit the needs of his, she had reached a state of near nervous breakdown which had culminated in her calling off the wedding and refusing to see Lucas.

'Unforgivable,' she murmured now. 'How could you have been so callous?' But she'd had to do it that way because otherwise Lucas would have talked her out of it—he'd tried to see her, tried to speak to her on the phone, even lurked where he'd hoped to run into her, but she'd woodenly refused to discuss it, and had been protected from him by her family.

She remembered with a sharp pang that Erica, the elder of her two stepsisters, had said matter-of-factly, 'Ten years from now you'll laugh about it, Lara. You'll laugh at yourself for believing you were in love! And you'll thank the rest of us for helping you to be sensible.'

Well, she wasn't laughing. She was crying inside, because she'd been wrong and they'd been wrong, and she'd lost the only man who was ever going to matter to her. And the irony was that both Erica and Jane, those two dedicated feminists, were now married with children and had both given up their careers. But she shouldn't blame them, she thought; she probably would have made the same decision without their pressure. At nineteen marriage was a big step, the future an unknown landscape, and she had been afraid and confused by the decision she'd had to make.

The doorbell rang and Lara, glad to be freed from her bleak memories, hurried to her date.

Lucas ran his eye over her appreciatively. 'Very nice,'

he drawled softly, desire flickering for a moment in his dark eyes.

She didn't ask him in. They were late enough as it was. 'Thanks,' she murmured, adding, 'It was nice of you to invite me, Lucas.' Was it only because neither Teresa nor any of the other women he probably took out were free this evening? She didn't spoil it by adding that.

'I want to talk to you about the ops coming up,' he said, giving her an alternative reason, which she ought to have been pleased about, but contrarily wasn't.

There wasn't much time for medical chat before the show, however, and at the interval they were accosted by a colleague of Lucas's and his very glamorous wife. Lucas introduced Lara to the Morrisons and, with a rather challenging look at her, told them, 'I'm trying to persuade her to give up being a hack and return to being a quack!'

'Ha, ha!' mouthed Lara, glaring at him as the others laughed.

'You shouldn't try to influence people where their careers are concerned,' said Isla Morrison seriously. 'I had a lot of pressure put on me to be a doctor when what I really wanted to be was a lawyer. My father was a doctor, you see, and so was my mother. My brother followed suit, but I had other ideas.' She laughed. 'I wasted two whole years as a medical student before I convinced everyone it wasn't for me.'

'Wasted?' chimed in her husband, Derek. 'You met me!'

Isla tucked her arm through his. 'Well, something good had to come out of it. You didn't want me to switch courses, remember, and we had terrible arguments about it. We nearly didn't get married.'

Lara felt Lucas's eyes on her but didn't dare look at him. Inside she ached unbearably because Isla and Derek had obviously solved their problem and she and Lucas had not. Isla would have been a very level-headed girl, she felt sure. She wouldn't have worried herself into a nervous breakdown.

The intermission bell rang and they started back to their seats.

'Is Derek at SCG?' Lara asked.

'Yes. He's in charge of the renal unit.'

'His wife's very attractive.'

'Clever, too. She has three kids and a thriving law practice.' To Lara it sounded like an accusation—or a reproach.

They edged along the row and sat down just as the lights began to dim. 'Enjoying it?' Lucas whispered, touching her thigh briefly.

'It's marvellous! I thought it might have been over-rated, but it really is wonderful entertainment.'

There was no time for more talk until the end of the show. Lara gave her whole attention to the spectacular musical drama on stage, now and then stealing a side-long look at Lucas, and every time she did his strong profile sent small shivers down her spine. Once he turned and smiled, and this small acknowledgement of pleasure shared was a poignant moment because they had shared similar moments so often ten years ago.

After the show they were on the footpath, about to walk to Lucas's car, when Derek Morrison called to them over the heads of the crowd pouring out of the theatre. He pushed through to them and said; 'How about some supper? We ate early and Isla's starving.'

Lucas glanced at Lara. 'We ate rather early too. What do you say, Lara?'

She was sure he wanted to go, so she agreed. It would add a little more precious time in his company, and they could chat about up-coming operations in the car going home just as well later as now.

'Bosco's then?' Derek suggested, and Lucas nodded.

The nightclub was only a few minutes' drive away on the fringe of the city. The Morrisons were waiting at the entrance when Lucas and Lara arrived, still enthusiastically discussing the show they had just seen.

'Wasn't it great?' Isla said, walking in beside Lara as her husband organised a table. 'I've been mad about the music for ages. I bought the compact disc the minute it came out. Have you got it?'

'No, but I think I'll have to buy it, I'm hooked!' admitted Lara. She felt very much at ease with the tall redheaded lawyer. Isla seemed carefree and easy-going, but there was a sharp intelligence under her casual manner. Lara felt sure she would stand no nonsense from anyone in court, judges included.

'When my wife becomes a High Court judge,' Derek was saying as they sat down, 'I shall retire and wallow in the luxury I was born to enjoy.'

'You'll be lucky!' Isla exclaimed. 'Women still have a tough climb in law. And it isn't much better in medicine, I bet.' She looked to Lara for confirmation. 'Was that why you quit, Lara?'

'No, it was just—well, circumstances,' Lara said evasively.

'She felt like a change,' Lucas put in with a rather hard look.

Lara didn't want to discuss her reasons for leaving the

medical profession, since it required leaving too much out, and there was always the danger that she would trip herself up. She was glad to see a waitress hovering, who switched their interest to food and drink.

To her relief, the subject of her career did not come up again. The men inevitably talked medicine, and Isla rolled her eyes and said to Lara, 'Don't mind me—I'm used to it.'

But Lara preferred to leave them to it and chatted to Isla about her work, which involved a good deal of legal aid, especially for women involved in family court cases. Some of her tales were very harrowing. Isla also talked about her family and was clearly very proud of her two sons and a daughter.

'I don't know how you manage to be a parent and run a law practice,' Lara marvelled.

Isla was dismissive. 'It's not so difficult once you've had a bit of practice. I didn't work while the children were young, but once they were out of primary school I went back to the law and, although it was hell at first, I got used to it.' She laughed. 'And so did they!'

Coffee was brought, and brandy, and then Derek said, 'Are we going to dance?' He looked at his wife and then at Lucas and Lara.

'I thought you'd never ask,' said Isla, sparkling. 'It is my birthday, after all!'

Congratulations followed this confession, and Isla leaned over and said in a low voice to Lara, 'It's not often I get the chance to smooch around a dance-floor with my spouse.'

They got up to dance, and Lucas looked a question at Lara, half standing as he did so. She went willingly enough into his arms, although she knew it would hurt.

To be held close by Lucas was bliss, but in her life now he was no more substantial than the memory. Even if— and it was a very big 'if'—he could forgive her for jilting him, there was still an insurmountable barrier between them. She would never be able to bring herself to confess to him her part in the scandal that had made her go overseas, and not to tell him was just as unthinkable. If you loved someone you didn't keep secrets from them, but to tell Lucas she had once been accused of stealing another researcher's results would require more courage than she possessed.

She had tried it. Twice. And each time she had suffered the kind of humiliation she had vowed never to bring upon herself again. When she'd met Andrew Sinclair, a physician working in London, she'd begun to think she might fall in love again. She had told him about the Lovell Institute fiasco in the firm belief that he would understand, would believe her, but, in spite of the proof, he'd still thought her tainted and had bowed out of her life very rapidly. She'd been shocked, and hurt, but had excused him on the grounds that his being a doctor might have made him wary. When she'd met Peter Granger, an engineer, she'd been confident of sympathy, but to her dismay Peter had faded out of her life too—before she'd even had time to fall in love with him. She had felt in her bones that it had been her confession which had precipitated his departure too. Feeling she would never rid herself of the stigma, she'd never told anyone else. She had decided it was better to stay single than risk humiliation like that again. If it was so hard for a man to trust her then there was no point in falling in love.

'You're trembling,' Lucas was murmuring in surprise as his arms folded around her. 'Cold?'

'No. . .'

'Can't be nerves, surely?' He smiled at her teasingly. 'You can't have forgotten how to dance.'

'Maybe the brandy's gone to my head,' she said, trying to sound light-hearted.

'It has given you a rather attractive glow,' Lucas said, and brushed his lips across her brow, drawing her closer as he did so.

The lighting was dim and the atmosphere intimate. Lara glimpsed Isla dancing with her head against Derek's broad chest and longed to do the same with Lucas, but dared not. But when his hand stole slowly up her spine, caressed her nape and gently pushed her cheek against him, she did not resist. It was so nice. . .so sensuous. . .so. . . A tear escaped and ran down her cheek into the corner of her mouth. What was she going to do, she thought, if when they got home Lucas wanted to come up with her? Was she going to let him? In spite of the hurt, was she going to let him make love to her? She knew she would be too weak to say no. You could easily say no when you didn't love a man, but when you ached desperately for even the tiniest part of him it wasn't so easy.

They left around two a.m. and Lucas was rather quiet on the drive home. Lara felt it wasn't quite the right moment to talk about operations and her series, so she was silent too. She was still wrapped in the joy of dancing with Lucas, of just being with him, and there was a quiver of anticipation jumping about inside her.

Lucas parked outside her block of flats and accompanied her up to her apartment. Lara's heart was thumping madly as she put her key in the door and opened it. She turned to face him.

'It was a lovely evening, Lucas,' she said softly. 'The show was fantastic. I really enjoyed it.'

'So did I.' He was looking at her strangely, as though half angry with her. What had she done to annoy him? she wondered, perplexed.

'I enjoyed meeting your friends,' she said.

'I'm sure they enjoyed meeting you.'

He's waiting, she thought, waiting for me to make the move. I've rejected him once and he doesn't want to be rebuffed again. If I want him now I've got to do the asking. But she couldn't. She couldn't bring herself to invite him in. Just one word from him and she would capitulate, but something deep-rooted in her wouldn't let her make the first move.

'Thanks for coming up with me,' she said. Then she smiled. 'We never did get around to talking about those operations you're going to let me observe.'

'No, we didn't.'

'Two-thirty in the morning is a bit late,' Lara said, dragging it out, wishing he would go or say something else. . .

'Do you have to be up early tomorrow?'

'Not particularly, but I do want to make a start on writing up my notes from today.'

'Of course. You won't forget I want to vet your material?'

'No.'

They looked at each other, with nothing more to say, and the tension was almost unbearable.

'I'll say goodnight, then,' Lucas said. 'Or rather, good morning.'

'Yes. . .good morning. And thanks again.' For our anniversary, Lara thought.

He started towards the stairs and was a few steps down when Lara felt the full impact of loss and disappointment. Scruples vanished and she heard herself call, 'Lucas. . .'

He stopped and turned round. 'Yes?'

Her colour was rising furiously, and she was trembling again, worse than in the nightclub. 'Lucas, you don't have to go. . .if you don't want to. . .' Her voice was barely audible, but he heard.

He came back up to the landing and stopped, facing her. For a long agonising moment he stood there, dark eyes devouring her, and then he said, 'But I think perhaps I should.'

A moment later he had gone and she was left without even an echo of his soft footfall on the carpeted stairway. He had gone! She couldn't believe it. She had weakened, she had invited him back, and he had rebuffed her!

Devastated, Lara fell back inside and closed the door. She staggered into her bedroom and flung herself face down on the bed, numb with defeat and humiliation.

CHAPTER EIGHT

To ensure that she survived the following week without betraying herself, Lara had to bring every fibre of her self-control into play. Away from Lucas, she schooled herself to behave normally, to keep the situation in proper perspective, and not to brood.

It won't be for much longer, she told herself. Once the heart-surgery series was written, she would never see Lucas again. Unless she heard he had moved on, which was unlikely, she would make sure that any story involving South City General was covered by someone else. She might even move on herself, she thought. Go back to Sydney maybe, or overseas again. There was nothing to keep her here. She had grown away from her family and seldom saw them, especially as her father and stepmother had now retired to Queensland. She might even practise again. . . This sudden awareness that her interest had shifted slightly from the detached observer to the involved medico made her smile a little. Once a doctor, always a doctor, Lucas would say, she thought, if she told him.

When Vera Turnbull rang to postpone the dinner invitation for a week, Lara could have believed that it was Lucas's doing if his mother hadn't so obviously had a heavy cold and she hadn't been so insistent on making an alternative date. Lara thought of making some excuse herself not to go, but she knew Lucas's mother would be suspicious and possibly jump to conclusions, right or wrong, so she decided to go through with it and try hard to behave as though nothing in the world was upsetting her.

Lara also steeled herself to attend the three operations to which Lucas had invited her, even though she was greatly tempted to pull out. But her professional commitment to the series made that unthinkable, especially with Grant still out of action and fretting about the series from his sick-bed.

Two of the operations Lara was to observe involved congenital heart disease in children; another was an embolectomy to remove a clot from a coronary blood vessel in a middle-aged male patient. None of them, she learned on her arrival at the hospital, was to be performed by Lucas himself, and, although Lara knew she should have been relieved, she was disappointed when she realised she would be watching other surgeons at work, and suffered some anguish because she suspected that his absence was deliberate. There was compensation, however, in that he had given permission to Dirk to take pictures on each occasion.

There was some delay before the first operation, and Lara found herself having coffee with Graham Butterworth, who was in the mood for personal confidences. He was a recent divorcee, she discovered, and obviously out on a limb. Feeling sorry for him, she agreed to a date because she felt neither of them expected anything would come of it. Graham, she suspected, for all his flirting, was still at the stage of needing a shoulder to cry on.

When Lara entered the theatre, to her surprise, Teresa Ioannidis actually smiled at her and seemed to go out of her way to be helpful. Lara guessed this to be because

Lucas must have reassured her that there was nothing between him and Lara.

Lara nevertheless took care that her presence was as unobtrusive as possible, and was relieved to find that the other surgeons were not in the least fazed by her presence.

The morning went well, and after lunch in the doctors' dining-room, accompanied by Graham Butterworth, Lara felt almost like part of the furniture.

'Doesn't it make you want to come back?' Graham asked, eyeing her with a challenging smile.

Lara shook her head. 'I like what I'm doing.' But she wasn't sure she was convincing him or herself.

She could not help letting her gaze rove around the room and, although she denied it to herself, she was looking for Lucas. He did not appear, and Lara was ashamed of keeping half an eye on the door and letting her pulse race every time it opened and someone came in.

As though he noticed and suspected the reason for her restlessness, Graham said, 'Lucas is off today. He had a big list yesterday. I half expected to see you, since there were a couple of cases I'm sure would have interested you. Couldn't you make it?'

Lara had the presence of mind to say, 'No—no, I couldn't. I'm doing another series on natural therapies. . .' She launched into a few details and so diverted the conversation from Lucas. She was sure now he had switched his schedule to avoid her.

But when she returned to the theatre suite, ready to observe the final operation of the day, she received a shock. Lucas was there.

Paling a little, Lara stammered. 'Oh—hello. I thought you were off today.'

He barely acknowledged her. He seemed preoccupied. 'We've had to postpone the last case. We're doing a more urgent one instead. It might interest you, however. A collapsed graft in a femoral artery. The patient had a bypass some months ago but the graft deteriorated. There are signs of gangrene.'

'It sounds ominous.'

He nodded. 'He may lose his leg. We'll try to prevent that, however.' He added, 'I did a coronary bypass on him, too, which is why I wanted to operate today.'

Lara was surprised, but accepted his explanation. It was no business of hers why he chose to do what he did. As though he had said all he intended, Lucas left her and she did not see him again until she was in the theatre waiting for the operation to begin. The patient, a sixty-five-year-old man, was conscious and, Lara quickly discovered, because of blood-pressure problems he was not to have a general anaesthetic but a lumbar puncture, which would paralyse the lower half of his body only.

As final preparations were being made Lara found herself taking over from the nurse who had been chatting to him and reassuring him. She was surprised when Lucas, evidently hearing her addressed as 'Sister', leaned over and said, 'She's a doctor, Tom, but she writes for *New Era* now, and you're her latest "copy", so watch what you say, or you might make headlines!'

Tom Rankin, the patient, was cheerful enough, but Lara sensed his underlying anxiety, and she felt for him, being, as she knew, about to undergo a lengthy operation. Sometimes it was better to be right out of it rather than be privy to all that was going on. Not that Tom could see much, since there was a screen across his body preventing that, but he could hear everything that was said.

'Keep talking to him, Lara,' Lucas murmured. 'Keep his mind off it. We can't hurry this one.'

Feeling suddenly like a part of the team, Lara did as she was asked and experienced an unexpected lift of spirits. With half an ear on what the surgeons and nurses were saying, she chatted to Tom about anything she could think of, including telling him what was happening, how the surgeons had previously used part of his own saphenous vein, but that as it had broken down they were now resorting to a synthetic material.

'You'll have to take it easy for a bit,' she told him. 'No heavy lifting or any activity that might cause the graft to break away. I know that'll be difficult for an active man like you, but it's essential if you're not to keep coming back for further grafts.'

He was very cheery to begin with, joking with her and the doctors and nurses, but, as time dragged by, Lara could sense his exhaustion. It was a long time to lie still, and she did her best to alleviate his boredom and impatience, but by the time the operation was completed, several hours later, she was feeling exhausted herself.

That was partly because all the time she was aware, too, of the closeness of Lucas. She was practically at his elbow, and every breath he took she seemed to be aware of it. When she happened to catch his eye, there was no reading his expression, and once, when she thought he smiled at her, she could not be sure because the mask concealed his mouth.

At last it was over and Lara could not wait to get away. She hoped to avoid Lucas, but he caught her as she was about to leave the theatre suite.

'You haven't forgotten Mother's invitation to dinner, I trust?' Lucas's deep tones startled her.

Lara wheeled round, trembling all at once. 'No, of course not.' She smiled. 'I'm looking forward to it.'

His eyes drifted languidly over her, their expression as unfathomable as usual, except for the flicker of masculine interest that always lurked there.

'Thanks for lending a hand today,' Lucas said. 'It was pretty gruelling for Tom, but talking to him as you did helped a lot. Your bedside manner is impeccable.' Lucas wasn't sure why he was being so amenable. In some perverse way he wanted to please her, and yet at the same time obstruct her. She was a real thorn in his side still, and he would be glad when this exercise was over. It was a pity, he thought, that he'd agreed to it in the first place, and then later let her boss keep him to his word. He was well aware he wouldn't have if he hadn't wanted the opportunity of seeing her again. But what had that achieved? Seeing her again, being close to her, had only tangled his emotions, leaving him in a state of ambivalence where she was concerned. Love. . .hate— he wasn't sure what he felt any more. And he sure didn't have a clue what she really felt.

Lara was wary, not knowing whether he was being sarcastic or for real. She changed the subject. 'I saw Jessica Price today,' she told him, knowing it was only an excuse to keep him talking. 'She looks very perky.'

He nodded. 'So does her mother!'

'Gives you a warm feeling, doesn't it,' Lara said slowly, 'knowing you've made life easier for someone, especially a small child?' She shrugged dismissively, wishing she hadn't made a remark he was bound to think sentimental.

To her surprise he said fervently, 'Yes, it does.'

Lara heard nothing further from Lucas until the day before she was to go to dinner at his mother's house. He phoned her at the office.

'I'll call for you about seven tomorrow. OK?' He was pleasant but peremptory.

'There's no need——' she began.

'I'll call for you,' he said firmly, adding, 'My mother would think me very ungallant if I didn't!'

Her resolve evaporated. 'Well, I wouldn't want to ruin your image with your mother,' Lara responded lightly. 'You're the apple of her eye!'

Lucas, as always, was punctual. When Lara opened the door to him he made no move to come in and she did not ask him. She felt quite calm and not nearly as apprehensive about the evening as she had earlier in the week. It was just a question of perspective, she had told herself over and over all week, and the advice seemed to have worked. Tonight she was having dinner with a couple of old friends, and there was no reason whatsoever to bring her emotions into it.

She had been in a bit of a quandary as to what to wear. Mrs Turnbull had always been rather formal, and as she was contemplating her wardrobe it suddenly occurred to Lara that she might not be the only guest. There might be others there, a real dinner party. Vera Turnbull had once loved giving dinner parties and had entertained her husband's colleagues and contacts a great deal, and if she was now emerging from her grief she might be venturing to do so again. Lara had not thought to ask Lucas and he hadn't mentioned it.

In the end Lara had chosen a cream wool dress with a double-breasted deep-collared bodice and a full skirt as being the most suitable of her outfits for the occasion. Lucas's approving eye confirmed her choice.

'Ready?' he queried.

'Yes.'

As she picked up her tan collarless jacket from the chair beside the phone, Lucas said, 'I should put that on if I were you. It's chilly out.' Before she could protest that it would be warm enough in the car so she probably didn't need it anyway he had taken it from her and was holding it out.

Lara slid her arms into the sleeves and allowed him to settle it, shivering at the feel of his hands brushing across her shoulders. She swallowed hard and gathered her bag and the gift of a posy and liqueur chocolates for Vera.

It was warm in the car, but Lara felt chill inside. Lucas's brief touch had left her feeling cheated. She wanted his arms right around her, holding her tight, his mouth hungrily devouring hers. She wanted him so desperately that she felt she would scream.

'You're tense,' Lucas stated.

'I'm not!'

He gave a short sceptical laugh. 'You won't have to suffer any recriminations, I assure you. I told my mother I wanted no delving into the past.'

'I'm sure you didn't have to do that. Your mother has impeccable manners.'

He did not answer the rebuke, but said, 'I'm sorry we haven't been able to give you a big one yet.'

'Big one?'

'A heart or heart-lung transplant.'

'You mentioned you had two candidates waiting.'

His voice was grim as he corrected her. 'One. The other died yesterday.'

'I'm sorry. . .that must make you feel bad.'

'Helpless. There's nothing we can do unless there's a donor.'

She felt his sense of failure keenly. 'How long has the other patient got?'

'A matter of weeks. We've had two possibilities but each time there was a problem—first incompatible blood type, then a deterioration problem caused by unavoidable delay getting the donor heart to the SCG.'

'It must be difficult for the patient,' Lara said slowly, 'knowing that someone else has to die to help them live. You wouldn't want to wish someone dead, but how could you help it?'

'I think Gerry Maguire might be prepared to talk about it,' Lucas said. 'If you'd like to talk to him.'

'I would! But. . . I don't want to invade anyone's privacy.'

Lucas shot her a quick cynical glance. 'I thought invading people's privacy was what journalism was all about.'

'Sometimes. Not always,' she defended. 'I don't agree with the way some stories are treated. I don't think people should be harassed. If they're willing—and you'd be surprised how many people are, even in tragic circumstances—then I see nothing wrong with interviewing them.'

'It can be ghoulish, even if they agree. Just because the public loves sensation it doesn't mean they should be titillated.'

'*New Era* doesn't titillate,' Lara said with some asperity. 'We're not a tabloid! I don't aim for sensation and my editor doesn't expect me to provide it. I write facts, and the embellishments are realistic.'

'Yes, I've noticed,' Lucas said, and as his tone was totally devoid of sarcasm Lara took that as a compliment. It mitigated his general disapproval.

Lucas drew up in the driveway to his mother's house. He turned to Lara. 'You still like a good argument!'

Hot colour stained her cheeks and she hoped it wasn't too obvious. 'Don't you?' she countered, with a pang beneath her ribs.

Spirited discussion was a better description, she thought, of the far-into-the-night debates that she and her fellow medical students had often indulged in, sometimes with more experienced members of the profession, and usually aided by a wine cask or a crate of beer. Oh, how long ago it seemed. And she and Lucas had enjoyed debating too, just the two of them. Their relationship had been cerebral as well as physical.

'So this is your mother's house,' Lara said, resolutely chasing memories away. 'What a lovely old place.'

'It's a little large for her,' Lucas said, a thread of anxiety in his tone. 'But she's determined to stay.'

'And it's a base for you.' Lara got out of the car and they walked to the front door together.

'For the time being anyway,' Lucas said, and Lara felt her heart contract. Living with his mother must place some restrictions on his private life. Was he hankering for the freedom a bachelor pad would afford? Or perhaps he was thinking of marriage. Maybe in the end Teresa would tame him.

Vera Turnbull must have heard the car arrive for she opened the door before Lucas had a chance to.

'Come in, come in!' she greeted Lara warmly. 'How lovely to see you again, my dear. Come and warm up—it's freezing out there.' She took Lara's arm and escorted her into the living-room, where, as Lara had half expected, a small group of people was already gathered. 'I asked a few friends to join us. Let me introduce you.'

Lara was glad that the company was not just Lucas and his mother. The other guests were professional people, one couple several years older than her, being university lecturers, and the other a retired businessman and his wife who were more Vera Turnbull's generation. They were pleasant, conversational and interested in Lara's work. It was flattering to find that they all read her articles and admired them. But, although she chatted happily enough to them before and during the excellent dinner Vera had prepared herself, Lara was uncomfortably conscious of Lucas's dark gaze following her. Her relief at not having to make small talk with him was somewhat dampened by this attention.

Finally, Vera urged them away from the dining table. 'Lucas, take everyone back to the living-room and offer them liqueurs while I make coffee.' The two older women made polite offers to help before Lara could get a word in, but Vera said firmly, 'Lara will give me a hand, won't you, my dear?'

'Of course.'

That it was a ruse on Vera's part to get her alone for a few minutes soon became evident. As she busied herself with the drip-filter coffee-maker, after setting Lara to slice a deliciously light cake and set out brandy snaps on a dish, she said, 'I hope you didn't mind my asking the

Harlingtons and the Granthams. I thought you all might find each other stimulating, and it was in the nature of an experiment.' She smiled wanly. 'My first dinner party since my dear Philip died.' Her voice shook for a second, then she regained control of herself. 'I knew I had to come back into the world some time. Grief is terrible, Lara; terrible. You want to run and run and run. It's like a gaping wound you think will never heal, but it begins to. . .'

'Don't. . . Vera, don't upset yourself,' Lara said gently. 'It's been a wonderful evening and you were very brave to take the plunge.'

Vera looked at her. The older woman's eyes were bright with unshed tears. 'Lara. . . I'm a silly old woman. . .'

Lara impulsively gave her a hug. 'You're marvellous!'

Vera clutched her hand. 'Lara, I'm getting on and I do so want to see Lucas settled down and happy.' She looked earnestly into Lara's face. 'It gave me real hope meeting you that day on the tram. Is there any chance that you and he. . .? You've been seeing quite a bit of each other lately, and you're older now. Is there any chance you're going to get together again? I would be so happy if you were.' She spoke the last sentence anxiously as though she wanted to dispel any possibility that Lara might think she would disapprove, and that that might be an obstacle.

Lara drew back, biting her lower lip. She had no alternative but to disappoint her hostess. 'Vera, I'm sorry,' she said. 'I'm afraid the answer is no.'

Vera's lips pursed. 'But you were so happy together once. Philip and I used to say what a grand pair you made. I know Lucas is quite a bit older than you and, although I was very angry with you at the time, I did understand why you jil—why you felt you couldn't go through with the marriage then. We both hoped you would get back together in time, but your ways parted and it seemed impossible until recently. Lara, I'm a great believer in fate and I'm sure fate has brought you together again for a purpose.'

'It was just one of those coincidences. . .' Lara faltered, shaking her head.

Vera's expression was stern. 'Are you still a career-woman, determined to remain single?'

'I'm not anxious to get married.' Liar, Lara chided herself. You'd marry Lucas tomorrow if it were possible. She added, 'I'm not sure Lucas is all that keen to marry either. Marriage means a lot of responsibilities.'

'Which, being doctors, you both know a lot about,' said Vera curtly.

'Maybe that's why we avoid taking on more, especially personal ones,' ventured Lara, refusing to consider Teresa in the role of Lucas's wife.

Vera scoffed. 'Nonsense! Most doctors get married. You're evading the issue, Lara.' She looked hard at her. 'Pride is a terrible thing. Is that the problem? Neither of you will admit you're still in love because you're too proud?'

'We're not still in love,' Lara insisted.

'You've got a funny way of showing it,' Vera said drily. 'The way Lucas looks at you—hardly takes his eyes off you, I should say—and the sly little glances you shoot at him wouldn't fool this slowcoach coffee-machine!'

Lara laughed. 'I think you're imagining things, Vera. Why don't you ask Lucas?'

'Lucas! He'd tell me to mind my own business. I can't ask Lucas *anything* personal. He's a dark horse, Lara, even with his own mother.'

'Well, I can tell you that Lucas is not interested in resuming any kind of lasting relationship with me.'

'You think he wouldn't take the risk?' Vera asked bluntly. 'Because he's afraid you might change your mind a second time?'

'I doubt if he's even thought about it. Our relationship ended ten years ago. A lot of water has flowed under the bridge since then, Vera.'

'But neither of you has married,' Vera said reflectively, 'and that is something I find highly significant.'

Lara was eager to end the conversation before she gave away her true feelings completely. 'Shall I take the food in? I'll come back and help you with the coffee tray.'

Vera looked at her with a grim kind of annoyance, but she gave up quizzing her with good grace. 'All right. I'll say no more, but I think it's a shame. . .'

Lara sailed out of the door and did not hear the rest of the sentence. Lucas caught her eye as she re-entered the living-room and half smiled. Vera was wrong, Lara thought. He looked at her that way because she still attracted him physically, but he wasn't in love with her. And she didn't want him to be. That would only complicate matters more.

'Coffee's coming,' she said, smiling around the gathered guests, and then going back to the kitchen.

Vera had set up the tray ready for her to take in. Hands on hips, she surveyed Lara morosely. 'I was hoping for a couple of grandchildren to brighten my twilight years, right here on my doorstep, not thousands of miles away like the others. Very selfish of me. I'm sorry if I was impertinent.'

'You weren't,' Lara assured her. 'I can't blame you for wondering—or for wanting it all to work out cosily, and I'm sorry it isn't like that.' Out of sympathy she found herself saying, 'But you never know, the grandchildren might not be too far away. Don't tell him I told you, but Lucas is very enamoured of one of his theatre nurses and she clearly adores him.'

Vera looked interested for a moment, then flagged. 'I couldn't count the times I thought he was seriously interested in a woman at last, and every time it petered out.' She gave a twisted little smile. 'While he was overseas, every few letters he would mention a new name. But there was never anyone he was serious about.' She smiled. 'I think you turned my Lucas into a philanderer!'

'Maybe it's just as well I let him go. We might have been divorced by now. Marriage might never have been right for him at all.'

'Oh you modern people are so much more complex than we were,' Vera said impatiently. 'Come on, let's give them their coffee.'

In the living-room, conversation flowed back and forth over a variety of topics. Presently, when Vera went out to refill the coffee-jug, Lucas followed her to find another bottle of brandy. Lara noticed that Lucas had drunk very little wine at dinner, and no spirits at all. He must be on call tonight, she thought. And corrected herself. Lucas was always on call. He was available whenever he was wanted, whenever his superior skills might be needed. He was first and foremost a surgeon, and his first priority was always human life. And this wonderful man could have been her husband, Lara thought, always by her side at parties and dinners, laughing and playing with their children, sharing happiness and sadness. Oh, he wasn't perfect; who was? He had his faults like anyone else, but tonight she wasn't looking at them. She was wishing she had married him.

When Lucas and his mother returned, Paula Grantham was saying how awful it must be to have dinner parties and other entertainments interrupted by emergency calls. As though it had been waiting for the cue, the pager lying on the coffee-table suddenly sprang to life and made them all start.

Lucas reached for it and said, 'I won't be a moment,' as he rose and went out to telephone the hospital.

'Poor man,' said Paula. 'I suppose he'll have to dash off into the cold and spend half the night fighting for some poor devil's life.' She smiled at Lara. 'I'm not surprised you gave it up for something a little more congenial.'

Lara could have said that wanting a more congenial life had not motivated her at all, ever, but Lucas returned and, looking at her, said grimly, 'I have to go. Do you want to come with me or let Mother get you a cab home? I'll be very late.'

'I'd like to come,' Lara said. 'If that's OK with you?'

'Let's go, then.' He glanced around the others. 'Sorry about this, folks. It was a pleasant evening. Catch up with you all again soon, I hope.'

Lara muttered goodbyes and thanked Vera hastily as she hurried after Lucas to the car.

'What is it?' she asked as she fastened her seatbelt. He looked more than usually perturbed, she thought.

'Massive coronary.' He paused for a moment, then said grimly, 'Teresa's father. Nick Ioannidis.'

'Oh, Lucas—I'm sorry.' The news hit Lara between the eyes. No wonder he was taut. Teresa's father, and the responsibility for the man's life was about to be placed in his hands. 'What a shock for them.'

'It's no surprise,' Lucas said grimly. 'He's already had two bypasses and I'm not sure he'll survive a third.'

'I suppose he's overweight and hasn't watched his diet,' Lara commented.

'Yes. It's strange, but back in Greece Greeks have a lower incidence of heart disease than here in Melbourne, even when they eat the same food.'

'Maybe stress is the factor. It's a faster lane here.'

'Maybe.'

'I was reading another new study the other day saying olive oil is beneficial in preventing heart attacks. But, like the findings on cholesterol, it's still not really conclusive, is it? The fact that people are different from each other counts too.'

'We've still got a lot to learn,' Lucas agreed. He drove fast, accelerating through amber lights, and within a few minutes they were in the hospital car park, arriving at the same time as two ambulances swung into the bay outside the casualty department.

'Looks like trouble,' Lucas commented, and as he spoke another two ambulances, sirens blaring, came through the gates. 'Real trouble.'

'Must have been a pile-up,' Lara said as they hurried inside and up to the cardiac floor.

The whole hospital seemed to be abuzz with a sense of urgency. Lucas strode off to see Mr Ioannidis and presently returned with Teresa and her half-hysterical mother. Teresa threw Lara a glance that was far from welcoming, and for a moment Lara thought she was going to object to her being there. As the girl wasn't wearing uniform, Lara guessed she was off duty. Not that they would let her scrub for an operation involving a near relative if it was avoidable. She wondered if Lucas would let her observe, always assuming she wanted to, or would he ban her on the grounds that it would be too emotional?

While Lara hung back a little there was a short clash of wills and Lucas won. Teresa retreated to look after her mother, casting stricken looks at Lara, who was to be allowed to stay.

His arm around the girl's shoulders, Lucas said soothingly, 'Don't worry, love. He's pretty tough, your father. We'll fix him up OK.'

Teresa mustered a smile of thanks. 'It won't be your fault, Lucas, if he doesn't pull through,' she said shakily.

Lucas beckoned to a nurse and drew apart for a few quiet words. The sister gently took charge of Teresa and her mother. Dr Vernon, the cardiologist, came in and spoke urgently to Lucas and the two of them went out. Lucas returned a couple of moments later. He looked intently at Lara for a few seconds, then said; 'Go and scrub up. You can assist me and get a real story for your paper.'

Lara was stunned. 'Lucas, I can't do that! I'm not staff. . .'

'It doesn't matter. You're a doctor, aren't you? The place is frantic tonight. There've been a couple of bad road smashes and a dozen people are requiring surgery. We're short-handed. So don't argue, there's a good girl.'

Lara did argue. 'I can't, Lucas! It's years since I

assisted at an operation. And I don't know much about cardiac surgery.'

He half smiled. 'Then what the hell have you been doing lately? Haven't you learned *anything*? Don't worry, you won't have to do much, only what I tell you. There'll be another surgeon with us, but Nick's in a pretty bad way and I may need an extra pair of hands. I think you'll do.'

Lara stared at him, deeply agitated and suspicious of his motive, yet moved that he was prepared to trust her. 'What are you trying to prove, Lucas?' Something to her? Or to himself?

'Prove? I'm just giving you the chance of a good story. You want to get close to the action—you might as well lend a hand. Now, hurry along. I'll fix the details.'

Who was there to raise objections? she thought. If Mr Turnbull wanted something it was up to him to make decisions. She ought to turn around and march off, Lara thought, staring after him; she ought to have refused point blank. How dared he order her around like this? She was sure he was dropping her in at the deep end for a very good reason.

But the thought also came that perhaps she was needed, that her small contribution might count, and if she walked out now she would know it had been for selfish reasons, putting herself before the patient. . . And, besides, Lucas trusted her.

'Damn you, Lucas,' she muttered as she went to do his bidding.

CHAPTER NINE

THERE was no time for Lara to feel nervous about participating in the operation. With all facilities geared up to cope with the emergency, there was only the shortest possible delay before the patient was brought to the theatre.

'It's bedlam here tonight,' the nurse who helped Lara into her gown, said. 'We've had to turn a couple of cases away because our ICUs are full and we haven't even got a spare theatre. I just hope someone else can take them.'

Lara murmured brief answers, but her mind was thinking ahead to what was surely going to be an ordeal in more ways than one. As she carefully pulled on the sterile gloves a strange sensation ran through her. It was almost like the very first time she had ever been in an operating theatre, except that all the automatic reactions she had been taught were being awakened and for the next few hours she would have discarded the cloak of journalism and be wearing the mantle of medicine.

She was pleased to find that the anaesthetist was Graham Butterworth, but she had not met Lucas's other assistant, Peter Ng, a young registrar of whom the scrub nurse whispered to her, 'Peter's going to be brilliant; you'll be interviewing him one of these days for some great contribution to surgery, mark my words.'

Lara hoped that Teresa knew the young Vietnamese doctor was assisting, and that she didn't know Lara was.

155

Teresa might be reassured by the former, but probably
not by the latter.

Graham was looking grim. Lara could only see his
eyes but she had learned long ago to read the eyes of
medicos in masks and Graham's conveyed pessimism.

'It's my guess the only thing that'll save this guy's life
is a transplant,' he said, his voice muffled by the mask.
'I reckon that's his only chance. If Lucas can patch him
up again tonight—and that's a big "if"— then it'll be a
case of waiting his turn. But I don't think he'll be able
to wait long.'

The patient was wheeled in, and for some moments
there was seeming chaos as all the high-technology
equipment required to keep him alive, while surgeons
would try to repair the damage to his heart and arteries,
was positioned and connected.

Lucas came in and there were low-toned conferences
between him and Dr Ng and the anaesthetist. Everything
seemed to be taking an inordinate amount of time as it
happened, Lara noticed, but a check of the clock told
her that mere minutes were elapsing.

Lucas glanced at her, but of all the medicos his dark
eyes were hardest to read. With a slight jerk of his head
he motioned her to a position opposite him near the
patient's head. Nick Ioannidis's chest was bared and
swabbed, and his fight for life was about to begin. Lara
gave a quick glance to the heart-lung machine, which
would continue to take over his blood circulation and
respiration while the operation was in progress. Life was
so fragile, she thought. There was hardly any tangible
sign of it in the inert body, the grey immobile face. One
moment it was there, the next it could be gone, and none

of their skills could bring it back. The spark that was life was so capricious, so elusive, so precious. . .

Lucas was taking a scalpel from the theatre sister. But before he had a chance to use it there was a diversion. The theatre door opened and a nurse drew their attention. Lucas looked around but showed no anger at the interruption. Graham also looked up sharply.

'One of the road-accident victims has just died,' said the nurse in an urgent tone. 'His next of kin have consented to organ use.' She paused only for an instant, then said, 'Mr Hawkins says his heart may be a match for this patient if you need it. It's no good for the others, I'm afraid. Can you let Dr Lewis know quickly because the Alfred could probably use it if we can't.'

The tension in the operating-room was palpable. Lara held her breath. Dr Lewis was the heart transplantation unit's co-ordinator and she had recently interviewed him as part of her series. She knew him as a man who would work with speed and cool efficiency to make sure that the donor heart was not wasted, even arranging to fly it by chartered jet to Sydney if necessary. But time was of the essence since it was not possible to preserve a heart for much more than five hours.

Lucas hesitated for only seconds. 'If it's compatible we'll use it,' he said evenly. He turned to the team around him and said matter-of-factly, 'I'm sorry, everyone, but there will be a short delay.'

The next few hours were the tensest time Lara had ever known, and the most incredible. She had never expected to participate, even in a minor way, in a heart transplant. And for all the time she was there in that brightly lit, busy operating theatre she never once thought about the article she would write. For the hours she was wearing the cap and mask, the gown and gloves she was a doctor and nothing else, and at the end of it she knew that that was what she still wanted to be. Journalism was only a stop-gap. Medicine was what she really wanted. But did she have the courage to go back? The courage to face the fact that someone, somewhere, some time, could confront her with the past?

As Peter Ng, with Lucas and a third surgeon who had joined them, supervising, inserted the last sutures to close the wound in Nick Ioannidis's chest, and, at Lucas's direction, Lara snipped them competently and confidently, she knew that if Lucas had set out to prove to her that practising medicine was her real forte, not writing about it, then he had finally succeeded tonight. She caught his eye briefly and didn't care that he could probably read the capitulation in hers.

It was much later in the coffee-room, when everyone was winding down, that Lucas—having seen the patient into Intensive Care and satisfied himself that all the systems were working and there were no complications—came over to her and sat on the arm of her chair, cradling a steaming cup of coffee in his hands.

'Weary?' he asked, sounding exhausted himself.

'A bit,' she conceded, giving him a wan smile. 'I'm out of touch with that kind of pressure.'

'You could get used to it again,' he said, dark eyes challenging her.

'You made me assist you on purpose, didn't you?' Lara said. 'You want me to go back to medicine. But why, Lucas? What difference does it make to you whether I practise medicine or push a pen for a living?'

He didn't have to answer. Teresa Ioannidis came in and approached them. Lucas rose to greet her.

'We just saw him,' Teresa said tensely. 'My mother said I must come and thank you for everything straight away.' She smiled a little apologetically. 'I can't believe he's actually had a transplant.' There was a tremble in her voice.

Lucas draped an arm reassuringly around her slim shoulders. 'He was lucky, Teresa. If there are no rejection problems he'll be back in the restaurant quite soon and he'll have the chance of a good life ahead. Otherwise I wouldn't have given him more than a few weeks, even with another bypass.'

'He'll be mad when he finds out,' Teresa said with a faint smile. 'He vowed he'd never let a surgeon stick another knife into him.' She looked adoringly into Lucas's face. 'I'm so glad it was you who performed the operation,' she said softly.

'I had two very skilled surgeons to help,' Lucas reminded her modestly. He smiled. 'We mightn't have the reputation of the Alfred yet, but we're catching up! The whole team proved its efficiency once more.'

But for Teresa it was Lucas alone who had saved her father's life, Lara thought. She was totally excluded for the moment. Teresa seemed hardly to have noticed her presence, and temporarily Lucas too seemed to have forgotten her. There was an intimacy in the way they stood talking that made Lara's heart ache unbearably. This was the last article she was going to do, she decided. After this one, which she hoped would be the high-point of the series, there wouldn't be much point anyway. She had all the material she needed. Please don't let Nick Ioannidis die, she prayed, but it was a prayer as much for her own sake as for the man and his wife and daughter. A happy ending to her story was essential, and she had a strong feeling she was going to get it. And maybe Teresa was too—a happy ending of a different kind. Tonight must have brought her and Lucas closer together.

'I must go,' Lara heard Teresa say. 'George has come to fetch us home. I must try and persuade Mum to get some sleep. She'll want to be back here first thing in the morning to see how he is.' She reached up and kissed Lucas's cheek. 'Thanks again, Lucas, for everything.'

He seemed a little embarrassed when he turned back to Lara. 'I hope to God the man recovers,' he said.

I bet you do, thought Lara. And if he does you'll be Teresa's hero more than ever.

Lucas glanced at the clock. 'I'll take you home.'

This time Lara did not protest or say she would get a cab. She knew Lucas wouldn't let her, and in any case she wanted to have this brief time alone with him. It would probably be the last time. She would finish her articles, send him copies for his approval, and then their paths would diverge once more.

But she would have changed. Her feelings in the operating-room tonight would not prove to be transient, she knew. She had made up her mind. If she was never going to know the true fulfilment of love then she was going to know the fulfilment of doing the only thing she had really ever wanted to do: practise medicine. Lucas had forced her to acknowledge it.

For the second time since she had met him again they drove home in the grey dawn light. There was a misty rain falling and the haloed street-lights looked unreal, the streetscape murky and unfamiliar. On the previous occasion Lucas had invited himself to breakfast, but Lara didn't expect him to do so this time. Not after having rejected her invitation to stay the last time he had taken her home. The bitter humiliation of that rejection still made her flesh creep.

Lucas parked outside her block of flats and Lara said, 'There's no need for you to come up with me.'

'No, I don't suppose there is.' He eyed her steadily. 'Unless you'd like to offer me breakfast again?'

Lara could not resist the chance to prolong being with him. 'Well, it is nearly breakfast-time. . .'

He smiled at her. 'If you fall asleep over your corn-flakes I'll tuck you up and leave instantly.'

He caught hold of her arm as they walked up the two floors to her flat, and the thought swept through Lara that perhaps after all he regretted having left her the other night. She was perplexed. She had only a short time ago witnessed tenderness between him and Teresa, so why was he keen to be with her now? Was he hoping she would be his therapy this morning? Some men needed sex to release the tensions of work, of grief, of fear, even of exhaustion. Was he hoping she would provide the emotional release that he could not ask of Teresa at the moment?

Inside the flat, she turned on the heating as it felt chill and damp. She offered Lucas more coffee, but he refused. 'Not yet.' Smiling, he drew her down beside him on the couch. 'Lara, there's something I want to tell you first.'

Lara felt the pain circling her chest. Not now, she screamed silently. Please, not now. There's no need for you to tell *me* you love Teresa. She stared at him, unable to find words to prevent him.

He reached for her hand and cradled it in his. His voice was so low when he spoke, so charged with emotion that she could barely hear him. 'I love you,' he whispered huskily. 'I've never stopped loving you, in fact.' His mouth tilted in a familiar ironic expression. 'I spent a decade trying to despise you, then when I saw you again it all crumbled to dust. I realised that you were the reason I'd never felt strongly enough about any woman to marry.'

'Lucas. . .' Lara was stunned.

'I thought it was still pretty hopeless, despite the fact that we still struck some pretty lethal sparks off each other. There was that guy, Dirk, for instance, and possibly others—your boss——'

'Grant? Don't be ridiculous. He's married.'

Lucas shrugged. 'So? You're attractive to men, Lara. Graham Butterworth is greatly smitten, as I'm sure you've noticed.'

Lara was shaking her head and trying to say no, but he wasn't looking and she seemed incapable of making any sound.

As though propounding an impossible theory, Lucas said, 'The extraordinary thing is that my mother is convinced that you still love me. She told me last night, out in the kitchen when I was fetching the brandy, that I'd be a fool if I didn't tell you how I felt.' He looked up at her and laughed wryly. 'I never told her I still loved you, so I reckoned if she'd guessed right about me, maybe. . .' His eyes were full of urgent appeal. 'Is there any chance she might be right about you, Lara? That none of these others means anything to you?'

Lara closed her eyes. This was not happening. She was dreaming. 'They mean nothing. . .' she whispered, 'but, Lucas. . .'

He grasped her upper arms, looking deeply and

anxiously into her face. 'Do you need some more convincing? I was angry and hurt when you jilted me, Lara. I told myself I never wanted to see you again, that you were worthless and shallow. I think the more deeply we love someone, the more denigratory we are when they let us down. I tried to hate you, but you stayed with me, a thorn in a corner of my heart, reminding me that I was not cured of you yet. When I met you again I tried to see you with detachment, I tried to keep you out of my life, but I couldn't. I wanted you—all the time—not just in my bed, but beside me as we had once planned. Lara. . .you're grown up now, things have changed. . .'

'And your mother says I'm in love with you,' said Lara, holding back her feelings, allowing them no rein whatsoever. 'That's what she wants, of course. She wants to put the clock back.'

'We can,' Lucas cajoled softly. 'We can, Lara, if we want to.' He touched her face with infinite tenderness and Lara felt her bones melting in her body as his eyes searched her face for the truth. But they couldn't put the clock back. There was one very good reason why they couldn't.

'I think you're fooling yourself,' Lara said because it hurt too much to believe him. 'This is why you made me help you last night, isn't it? You're trying to prove that I really want to be a doctor, because that is an acceptable justification for jilting you. It hurts your pride too much to think that perhaps I was just a fickle woman where careers and men were concerned. . .that I still am. . .'

He looked shocked. 'Are you trying to tell me there was another man?'

Lara was distraught. 'No! There wasn't anyone. . . I didn't mean that.' She looked at him helplessly. 'It's no use, Lucas. Too much water has flowed under the bridge, as I told your mother. We can't go back and start again.'

Lucas took her hands in his, caressing her fingers. 'The other night, Lara, you called me back. . . Why?'

She felt the heat rise in a tide through her face. 'A weak moment. . .'

'It was one of the hardest things I've ever done, leaving you that night,' he said. 'I went because I knew that to stay would be letting you break my heart all over again. Then when my mother said——'

'I told you, your mother doesn't know what she's talking about,' Lara said hurriedly. 'Wishful thinking, Lucas.'

'You haven't answered my question, Lara. Do you still love me?'

He held her fiercely against him, and her heart pounded like a sledge-hammer in her chest. When Lucas's mouth touched her she shuddered as the desire his touch evoked shafted deep inside her. But she wouldn't answer.

'Lara. . .?' he challenged her again, and when she remained silent he sought her answer another way.

His hands raked her hair and caressed her nape, slid down her spine and drew her thighs hard against his. His mouth burned hers with a kissing like none she'd ever known since Lucas, and his tongue pressed gently into the warmer, more sensuous privacy beyond her lips, skilfully arousing her response so that she was scarcely aware of her arms encircling his neck and wildly holding him closer.

She was too intoxicated by him to protest when he scooped her up and carried her into the bedroom. She looked at him dreamily from under heavy lids, as though drugged, as he slowly undressed her, reverently caressing her body as each part was revealed, smiling at her with a kind of triumph in his dark eyes. Then his own clothing was discarded and he was gathering her close, fitting her slender body to his, caressing her skin with light arousing strokes that gradually became more urgent.

She felt she was floating on air as he pulled her down on to the bed. His lips teased her mouth with promises, took her hardened nipples with an exquisite torture and explored her body with the familiarity she had subconsciously yearned for all these years. She had never wanted to make love with any other man because instinctively she had known it could never equal, let alone surpass, making love with Lucas. If only she had realised that. . .if only she had known the heartache that giving him up would bring to her. . . And now, when he wanted her back, she couldn't go to him. She could tell him the truth, of course, but what if he rejected her?

Numbly she heard Lucas mutter her name as they came together at last, gasping and clinging, swept up on a wave of ecstasy that finally reached its pinnacle and then gently floated them down.

Lucas buried his head in her shoulder, his breath fanning her heated skin and his heart pounding against hers. Lara clung to his warm, moist body and let the tears run down her cheeks.

Lucas lifted his head slightly. 'You are splendid,' he breathed, not noticing the dampness on her face.

Lara smiled and touched his face. 'We shouldn't have. . .'

'Oh, yes, we should,' Lucas replied contentedly. He settled himself comfortably with his head on her shoulder and an arm and leg thrown across her. In a moment he was breathing the deep regular breaths of a man asleep. He was confident that he had the answer he wanted.

Lara lay rigidly for some time, unable to sleep herself, yet reluctant to disturb him. She pulled a sheet and blanket over them, and, as the extra warmth seeped through her, she became drowsy and slept too.

She woke to find Lucas propped on one elbow, looking down at her. 'As beautiful as ever,' he murmured. And, kissing her lips, 'Tell me now you don't love me.'

'Is isn't that. . .' she said, and almost told him, but it was too hard. It was better to have this bliss to remember than to risk the hurt and humiliation of seeing doubt cloud his love. If men she had never hurt in any other way had doubted her integrity and had faded off the scene as soon as they knew, then Lucas was even more likely to reject her. She was more than convinced that he would.

'If you want to come back to medicine,' he coaxed, caressing her warm relaxed body absently, 'I would never stand in your way, Lara. I never would have done. You had no need to be afraid.'

'No, I can't,' she said. 'I just can't, Lucas.'

'Why not?'

'Things are different now.'

'But you love me. And I love you. We belong together. . .'

Lara sighed deeply. 'You're just trying to salve your hurt pride, Lucas. You're trying to pretend I never jilted you. Perhaps your ego needs to do that. But it wouldn't work. It would be too much of a risk.'

'Don't you trust yourself?' he asked. 'Are you afraid you'd get cold feet again?'

'Aren't you?'

He rumpled her hair. 'No, my darling, I'm not. You're an adult now. You know your own mind.'

'Do I? I thought you had to show me!'

He looked at her strangely. 'When I first saw you again I tried to tell myself you were still fickle, still didn't know what you wanted, and therefore I'd be best to steer clear of you, but then I told myself I was being unfair.'

'Were you? You don't know that,' Lara said, deliberately feeding his doubts. 'I think you'd be happier with Teresa,' she added, wondering where she'd got the courage to say it.

'Teresa?'

'It's obvious she adores you. And I get the impression you're not entirely immune to her. There are no shadows in the past to mar your happiness.'

Lucas's slight rise in colour betrayed him, and Lara felt a sharp pang, remembering that day she'd seen him embrace the girl in his office. And their intimacy only a few hours ago had indicated a relationship beyond the call of duty.

Lucas answered gruffly, 'She's a good-looking girl, and I've taken her out a few times. But that's as far as it goes. I haven't even slept with her!'

Lara wasn't sure she could believe that. 'But you've been home to meet her parents.'

He sat up, raking his fingers through his hair. 'Yes, a couple of times. Teresa was worried about her father. He was deteriorating, but he was refusing to have further surgery, so in desperation she begged me to try and persuade him. Although I wasn't optimistic about another bypass, I did my best to change his mind, but he was adamant. He said he'd had enough.' He gave a short laugh. 'For heaven's sake, Lara, I didn't go because of any serious intentions towards Teresa!'

'You seemed to have a pretty serious intention about Teresa the day I came back to your office to fetch my umbrella.' She was gratified to see his look of alarm. 'I'm afraid the door was half open and I couldn't help seeing. . .well, a pretty intimate embrace.'

Lucas looked uncomfortable. 'I remember. I remember because it was the only time. You'd set me so much on fire that I was in the mood to seduce any female who crossed my path—out of vengeance! Teresa came in and was in a flirtatious mood. I'm ashamed to say I forgot myself for a moment. But it didn't go far. I was mortified when I found the door ajar, in case anyone had seen. I never dreamt *you* might have come back!' He looked puzzled as a memory surfaced. 'But someone came up for your umbrella, as I recall.'

'I could hardly interrupt that tender little scene,' Lara said, 'so I crept away again. I would have got wet if I hadn't run into Josh Edwards. He sent a receptionist to fetch the brolly for me.' She paused for a moment, then reminded him, 'Last night you were very tender with Teresa.'

He laid a palm on her cheek. 'And you were jealous?' he said softly. 'Lara, her father was near death; she was distraught and needed comfort. What else could I do but try to reassure her?'

'She's in love with you.'

'And I'm not in love with her!' He patted her face in exasperation. 'So you think I'm a philanderer. Is that the problem?'

'I don't imagine you've spent the past ten years celibate.'

'You surely don't think I would continue to take other women out if I married you?' He sounded shocked.

'I don't know what to think,' Lara said, wondering why she was even arguing about it. 'I just know that I don't want to take risks. I don't want either of us to take risks. Maybe you were too impulsive the first time—it might not have lasted. You seem to like being fancy-free. Maybe you're still attracted to young women. Teresa isn't much older than I was then. . .'

His eyes narrowed. 'Now you're being insulting.'

'Realistic.'

He sighed wearily. 'The truth is you're still afraid. Still afraid to commit yourself.'

'Yes, I suppose I am.' It was so easy, Lara thought, to sound convincing.

'You feel safer having an affair with that photographer character,' he accused, and, eyes glittering, 'or that workaholic boss of yours!'

If she hadn't been angry Lara might have laughed. 'I'm not having an affair with Dirk! Or Grant! Nor do I want affairs with either of them. Or *anyone*!'

Lucas felt his jealousy abating. Her vehemence was genuine and he was tempted to believe her. He *wanted* to believe her.

He clasped her hands tightly. 'Lara, life is a risk. You can't play safe all the time. You have to commit yourself to all kinds of things and just hope sometimes it will turn out all right.'

She did not answer and he slid his arms under her, lifting her hard against his sinewy body, in an instant starting up the desire that again threatened to consume her. 'I'm going to make love to you again,' he said huskily. 'All right?'

It was all right. It was wonderful, and Lara lay in his arms afterwards, pretending the world outside had ceased to exist. She wanted to go on making love with Lucas for ever and ever, for there to be nothing else to do or matter except their being close and warm and loving. But love unfortunately had more realistic dimensions and wasn't as simple as one would like it to be.

Afterwards Lucas raised himself on his elbows and looked into her face. 'Well. . .?' He traced the shape of her mouth with a fingertip then his lips. 'Lara. . .?' A world of pleading was in his voice, and Lara resisted it with difficulty.

'I'll make us some breakfast,' she said, and swung herself out of bed. 'Have a shower if you want. I'll bring you a towel.' She donned a dressing-gown and slippers and padded out to the kitchen.

Lucas did not try to stop her and did not say anything. He felt the chill wind of defeat.

Lara heard the shower turned on and hooked a towel over the bathroom door. By the time Lucas emerged breakfast was ready.

Lucas did not mention their relationship. He had realised, as the stinging force of the shower turned full on had whipped his body, that arguing with Lara would be futile. She had deliberately and cold-bloodedly shut him out. She might have enjoyed making love to him, might have been unable to help herself, but she did not love him. His mother was wrong, after all.

They ate breakfast companionably enough, and over a second cup of coffee, for the sake of normality, he told her a few more background details about the previous night's surgery, and she jotted down notes.

Finally he said, 'I'd better be going.' He stood close to her and cupped her face in his hands. 'I guess we've said all there is to say.' He looked resigned.

It was painful to answer him. 'Yes, we have,' Lara said. 'I'll send you my copy as soon as it's finished. I'd like your comments as soon as you can give them.'

'I'll do it straight away,' he answered, and dropped a kiss on her mouth that momentarily became passionate, and then he gained control of himself and lifted his lips smilingly. 'I guess we'll have to leave it at that.'

'I guess so.'

After she had shown him out Lara returned to the kitchen and sank down at the table, her head on her arms, and dissolved into bitter tears.

CHAPTER TEN

'So you've just about wrapped it up?' Grant Jermyn said, popping an indigestion pill and giving Lara a defiant look as he did so.

He was supposed to be convalescing still, but he kept turning up at the office for an hour or two, refusing to listen to Lara or anyone else when they tried to advise him. Lara had stopped trying to dissuade him, and, like his wife, Nora, had resigned herself to the fact that Grant would always do what he wanted to do, no matter what the cost to his health.

She said, 'Just about. I've got a couple of follow-ups to do on the heart-transplant patient, that's all. Mr Ioannidis has agreed to talk to me as soon as the doctors permit it. Of course, I have to let Mr Turnbull see the copy. That was a condition of my being allowed to observe and write up the ops.'

Believing Teresa would be against it because of personal antagonism towards her, Lara had half expected Teresa's father to refuse to be interviewed. But Teresa herself had told Lara he wanted to help and she had seemed a little less hostile, if still cool. Perhaps, Lara thought, Lucas had turned to her after all. She still couldn't believe he'd meant what he'd said that morning after the operation. They'd both been keyed up, and the emotional charge between them had been high.

'You sound as though you'll be glad to be shot of the

assignment,' Grant observed with his usual sharp perception. 'What's the problem? Did you fall for the surgeon and get the brush-off?'

'You put things so diplomatically!' laughed Lara, no longer fazed by the blunt and sometimes abrasive approach used by her boss. She decided it was time for a succinct no-frills announcement herself. 'I'm quitting, Grant,' she said. 'I'm going back to medicine.'

He made an explosive sound that might or might not have contained an expletive. For all his outspokenness, Grant never swore in front of women. He reached for the bottle of indigestion tablets.

'What did you say?' he demanded, eyes narrowed, mouth aggressive.

'I said I'm quitting journalism and going back to being a doctor.'

He sucked on the tablet noisily. 'That's what I thought I heard. Why, for heaven's sake?'

'Because I got so close to it again doing this series that I realised it was where I really wanted to be. Writing about it isn't the same as doing it.'

'Why did you ever give it up?' he asked. 'Did you kill somebody?'

Lara reeled. 'Good grief, no!' She had half a mind to tell him about her disastrous year in MS research, but he didn't have the time, and she wasn't looking for sympathy. Not that she'd get it from Grant. So she said, as she'd said before to him as well as everyone else, 'I lost my sense of vocation temporarily. Overwork probably caused it.'

Grant grumbled loudly, 'So what am I supposed to do for top-notch medical reporting? When are you planning to desert me?' No recriminations. That wasn't Grant's style. He wouldn't try and persuade her to stay. He expected people to make their own decisions and to know what they were doing.

'I'll give the usual notice. One month, isn't it?'

He nodded impatiently. 'You could still write,' he said. 'Nothing unethical about that. You use a pseudonym.'

'I doubt if I'll have much time,' Lara said, 'but you can always ask me.'

His expression softened. 'I'm sorry, Lara. I like your work and so do the readers. You'll be missed.'

For Grant it was an emotional speech and Lara was touched. 'Thanks.'

'You'd better put your resignation in writing,' Grant said. 'Give it to me and I'll see you get everything that's due to you.'

'Thanks again.'

He looked hard at her. 'If the final piece is as good as the stuff you've shown me so far it'll be a great swan-song.'

His telephone rang and he barked into it. Lara rose and left. The deed was done, she thought as she went back to her office. Now all she had to do was plot the next part of her course. Would she stay in Melbourne and risk seeing Lucas, as well she might from time to time, or would she go back to Sydney? No, she thought, I can't do that. Perth or Adelaide maybe, or perhaps she would go overseas again. A year or two on voluntary service in a Third World country would distance her from Lucas, from the past, from everything. She might even write one or two specials for Grant. . .

She was still pondering the future when Dirk came in. She told him what she'd told Grant. He nodded as though not very surprised, and said glumly, 'I suppose this means you're going to marry Turnbull?'

'I am not! Whatever gave you that idea?'

He smiled a little wistfully. 'I only saw you together a couple of times but it stuck out a mile that there was strong chemistry between you. Boy, did I feel a champion gooseberry that night I called at your flat and put a wet blanket over the passion scene.'

Lara struggled to keep up the pretence. 'Dirk—you've got it all wrong. I'm not about to marry anyone. I don't think I'm the marrying kind. As a matter of fact, I'm thinking of going off to darkest Africa or South America or somewhere. I saw an advertisement the other day for overseas volunteers.' She saw his puzzlement and realised she hadn't explained properly. 'I'm giving up journalism and going back to being a doctor.'

He let out a long breath as a slow whistle. 'How about that? Well, I guess it was always on the cards. When are you leaving?'

'I've got to give a month's notice.'

Dirk considered her for a moment, then said, 'How about celebrating your decision tonight?'

Lara hesitated only for a second, then said, 'Yes, why not? What do you suggest?'

'Dinner and the Trombone Jazz Club? Galapagos Duck are playing.'

'Sounds great.'

Dirk said carefully, 'I suppose there's no chance for me. . .?'

Lara shook her head and said gently, 'I like you a lot, Dirk. I'm fond of you, but it isn't love.' She added, 'If you want to retract the invitation. . .?'

'Don't be daft. I like your company, Caro. I wouldn't

mind something more, I admit, but that's OK.' He eyed her speculatively. 'That Turnbull guy needs his head read to let a woman like you get away. What's the problem? The attractive dark-haired girl I saw him with at a Greek restaurant a couple of days ago?'

Lara flinched. 'There is no problem, Dirk. If Lucas marries Teresa—that's who you saw him with—it's no odds to me.'

Dirk saw that it was, but he said nothing.

Fortunately, Lara had a lot of work to complete before her notice was up. She interviewed Mr Ioannidis again at length, and Dirk took more pictures. It was a revealing interview. Having been at death's door and surviving now because someone else had died had had a profound impact on Nick Ioannidis, and, having had plenty of time during his convalescence to think, he was eager to talk about it.

His accent was thick, but Lara followed his words fairly easily, and had her tape to check back on later. Unlike some interviewees, he hadn't minded her tape-recording the interview. What Teresa really felt about it Lara did not know, as she only encountered the nurse once when she arrived to visit her father just as Teresa was leaving. Teresa had been polite but distant, and had not commented. It occurred to Lara that she might have swallowed her objections because Lucas approved.

Lara also checked on the other subjects she had written about, and compiled a follow-up piece to show how they were all getting along several weeks after their surgery. Everyone was co-operative. Judge Allardyce's wife invited her to lunch, and she paid a visit to the pre-school that Jessica Price attended. One way and another she caught up with all her subjects.

Lucas had already approved her first two articles, but she had not shown him the remainder yet. She had not, in fact, seen him face to face since the morning after Mr Ioannidis's heart transplant. He did not yet know of her resignation from *New Era* and her decision to return to medicine. She hadn't mentioned it to Josh Edwards yet, although she intended to eventually.

Whether she could summon the nerve to see Lucas to tell him that his effort to get her to return to medicine had succeeded she wasn't sure. Part of her longed to see him just one more time, but part of her knew that it might be better not to. A thank-you letter would be less distressing than a personal confrontation.

One task was proving difficult to complete: the article about the transplant. There was too personal an element about it, and when she was working on it she kept seeing images of Lucas before her eyes, and she would become so restless and unable to concentrate that she would have to put it to one side.

There was also the feature on natural therapies which she had promised to do, and gathering information for that occupied a good part of her day. She was still receiving a steady mail, too, which had to be answered, and her in-tray at *New Era* was also crammed with Press releases and other material that had to be read and sorted.

Disciplining her emotions as well as her mind, she finally managed to finish her heart-surgery article late one night, and, as she clipped together the pages of the copy she would send to Lucas for approval, and sat staring at it, something suddenly snapped inside her.

Maybe he had meant it when he'd said he loved her. Maybe her rejection had sent him reluctantly into

Teresa's arms. Maybe her confessioin would not have had the same disastrous outcome as before. . .

'Don't be foolish,' she told herself. 'That's wishful thinking. He doesn't really love you.'

But all at once she was possessed with an overwhelming urge to tell Lucas all about her disastrous year at the Lovell Institute, the scandal, everything about it, regardless. Suddenly it seemed imperative that she did. If only Lucas believed in her integrity, whether he loved her or not, she could shake off the awful guilt that had haunted her. If you've got the courage to be a doctor again you've got the courage to tell the truth to Lucas, she told herself.

Lara's hands shook as she slid the print-out of her article into an envelope and wrote Lucas's name on the front of it. Then she went to the drawer where she kept another envelope that she had not looked into for years. She shook out the Press cuttings, the correspondence, the report of the inquiry, and shivered. She would tell Lucas her story, and give him the evidence. Let him be her judge.

She hardly slept for imagining the confrontation. When she did she dreamed conflicting dreams, in one of which Lucas held her in his arms and tore her Press cuttings into tiny pieces, and in the other turned his face away in silent rejection.

The next morning, in spite of her dreams, she was still resolute, although a little nervous, when she telephoned to make an appointment to see Lucas. To her chagrin she was told he was away, giving a lecture in Sydney, and wouldn't be back for a couple of days. Lara felt all her courage ebb as she put down the phone. Maybe she wasn't meant to tell him. Maybe she would suffer less if she didn't. She took the large manila envelope containing the copy marked for his urgent attention to the hospital. The envelope containing the Press cuttings she put back in the drawer.

Three evenings later Lucas telephoned her at home. Her heart leapt, but in the intervening days her courage had ebbed and she wasn't sure she could broach the subject now.

'There are a couple of things I want to discuss.'

He sounded brusque, which didn't help, and with a sinking heart Lara knew she did not have the courage to tell him over the phone what she had intended. She swallowed hard and said, 'Can you wait while I fetch my copy?'

'I think I'd better come round,' Lucas said. 'It'll be a lot easier to explain in person.'

Lara moistened her lips nervously. 'All right, if you think that's necessary. When?'

'Right now, I thought. If you're not busy.'

'No. That's OK.' She was trembling so much that she could hardly hold the receiver.

He rang off and Lara tried to get a grip on herself. Somehow she had to maintain a composure she did not feel. She put coffee-cups out and ground some beans, sliced a small ginger cake she'd bought that day, and then paced up and down nervously until he arrived. The sound of his familiar ring at her doorbell made her mouth go dry and her knees weak.

She opened the door, hardly daring to look at him. 'Come in.'

He followed her into the living-room and sat down,

placing the manila envelope containing her articles on the couch beside him.

'Would you like some coffee?' she asked.

'Thanks.' He smiled, but his expression was unfathomable. Then he said, 'Don't look so wretched! There's nothing wrong with your articles. The transplant one in particular is brilliant.'

'But you said——'

'There are a few things I want to discuss. It won't take long.'

'I'll get the coffee,' she muttered, and fled.

In the kitchen Lara clung to the edge of the bench-top until her knuckles were white. Tell him! shrieked one voice in her head. No! screamed another. If you don't you'll never know, argued the first voice. Tell him and take the consequences. Lara closed her eyes in dread but she listened to the second voice.

When she came back and handed him his cup and offered the ginger cake, he said, 'You're like a cat on hot bricks, Lara. What's the matter?'

She sank her teeth into her bottom lip hard, then before her courage could desert her she plunged in. 'Nothing. Well, yes, there is something I want to say to you. . .tell you. . .'

He studied her carefully. 'It wouldn't by any chance be about something that happened to you several years ago? At the Lovell Institute?'

Lara drew in a sharp startled breath.

He went on, 'When you were part of a team researching MS.'

Lara covered her face with her hands. 'You know! How did you find out?'

'Quite by accident. One of the theatre nurses here has

a brother who is a cardiologist at the Southern Cross, whom I know quite well. While I was in Sydney I delivered personal greetings for her, and we had lunch. In the course of conversation Brett mentioned that Kate had told him about you and what you were doing now.'

'You're talking about Kate Gordon's brother, aren't you?' Lara said slowly. 'I don't remember him, but there were so many doctors. . .'

'He remembered you, though,' Lucas went on. 'Not from when you were an intern. . .' he paused and then, looking steadily into her stricken eyes, said, '. . .but from your time with the MS research team at the Lovell Institute.'

Lara could not speak. She wanted to tear her eyes away from him but couldn't. A gamut of emotions was spinning her heart and mind into turmoil. He already knew!

'Why didn't you tell me about it?' Lucas asked half angrily.

Lara found her voice, a small hesitant sound. 'It was something I wanted to forget.'

'I think you should tell me about it now.'

'You already know——'

'I know what Brett Gordon remembered, and what I searched out in medical journals and newspaper files. There wasn't a lot. Now I'd like to hear your side of the story.'

Lara moistened her lips nervously, her recently rehearsed explanation wiped from her mind. 'It's more or less as you read it in the Press. I was part of a team studying brain tissue from MS victims. We were each studying a different aspect, looking for a clue as to why the immune system in multiple sclerosis sufferers seems to produce cells which attack nerve cells in the brain. I was there for about a year and I happened to be lucky enough to achieve a minor breakthrough. It really was pure luck, considering my tyro status. The team's head researcher, Dr Christoff, unknown to me, released my findings to the Press. It was no big deal, no imminent cure was suggested, but the Press, on a slow day, beat it up a bit. It would have faded instantly, like many other such stories, if one of my experienced colleagues, who had been with the unit for several years, hadn't written a scathing letter to the newspapers and the medical journals, denouncing me as having passed off his research results as my own.'

Lucas watched her face impassively. Lara forced herself to finish the story. 'There was an investigation. Although the investigating committee found that the evidence wasn't conclusive one way or the other, I was nevertheless exonerated. We both resigned. I suppose the accusation on his part stemmed from a simple case of jealousy because I was the newest and youngest member of the team, and Dr Christoff had used my work to attract a little publicity and more funds.' She smiled ironically. 'A young female in a white coat who had gone into research because her mother had died from MS was good copy.'

'And that's why you went overseas?'

'Yes. I couldn't stay with the research job after that, and I felt too stigmatised to go back to practising in a hospital. It was a very salutary experience, so I packed my bags and went to the UK, where the chances of anyone knowing about it were negligible.'

'But it preyed on your mind, so, when the opportunity arose to quit medicine, you did?'

Lara gave a wry smile, spreading her hands helplessly.

'After your ordeal, I'm surprised you took up journalism,' Lucas said.

Lara had never considered that, and looked surprised now. 'I didn't blame the Press. It was all just a horrible mistake.'

'Why didn't you tell me?' Lucas asked again. 'You surely didn't think it would make any difference?'

Lara looked bravely into his face. 'I was afraid to. I had told other people—people I was fond of—and it had made a difference. Where there's smoke there's fire—you know the saying. My character was tainted. They weren't totally convinced. They only had my side of the story. It didn't make me easy to trust.' She covered her face briefly, then said, 'It was terrible sometimes. I would dream that I *was* guilty, that I *had* stolen someone else's results and pretended they were mine. I would wake in a cold sweat, certain it was true, overwhelmed with guilt and shame. I almost came to believe I was guilty even when I wasn't dreaming!'

Lucas moved suddenly and gathered her into his arms. 'Lara. . .oh, Lara. . .and you thought I would be like the others, that I wouldn't accept your word. Even when I told you I loved you.'

'I didn't. . .was afraid to believe you did. I was afraid to even risk humiliating myself again. You already had plenty of reason to distrust me. I jilted you. I still appeared to you like someone who chopped and changed, blew hot and cold, and wasn't emotionally or any other way reliable. I didn't want to give you another reason to despise me.'

He held her close. 'You've always been afraid, haven't you? You have too much self-doubt, not nearly enough confidence in yourself.' He tilted her face and looked a little wistfully into her eyes. 'Ten years ago you were afraid to marry me in case it spoiled your career, in case I fell out of love with you, and in case you fell out of love with me. You were afraid to begin again because you thought I was a philanderer and because you thought I'd never trust you again. Lara, my love, you can't expect to *know* how life will turn out, how people will behave. You have to take some chances. As we sometimes have to do in medicine—risks that may save a patient, or may not.'

'I have decided to take a chance,' Lara said softly. 'I'm going back to medicine. I'm not going to hide behind a pseudonym and another career. I'm going to be Dr Montague again. I've already resigned from *New Era*.'

Lucas looked astounded, then delighted. He hugged her. 'You have? That's wonderful! It's what you really want to do, isn't it? That journalism stuff was just because you were afraid of people finding out about you.'

'Yes.'

He was smiling broadly now. 'What are you going to do? General practice? Hospital work? Or back to research?'

Lara said faintly, 'Not research. I never really wanted to do that, but I felt a kind of obligation to take on the MS job because of my mother. No, I was thinking of volunteering for work overseas in developing countries—for a while, anyway. . .'

He shook her slightly. 'That would be running away and hiding again!'

'I know but. . .things being the way they were with you. . .'

'You mean because you love me?'

Her voice was a whisper. 'Yes. . .'

He laid his cheek against hers. 'Lara, it's very noble of you to want to go and help in the Third World, but I can't have my wife gallivanting off to the other end of the earth when I need her here.'

'Your wife?'

He captured her face in his hands again. 'Yes, my wife, and this time I'm going to get you to the altar before you have a chance to get cold feet.'

'Sounds like a *fait accompli*,' said Lara as a wave of happiness began to creep warmly over her.

'You bet it is.' He kissed her lips lightly. 'You are still in love with me, aren't you? My mother was right.'

'She was. I tried not to be, but it didn't work. When we met again I soon realised what a terrible mistake I'd made not marrying you, but I thought it was impossible to start again. I thought you liked being fancy-free or that you were in love with Teresa, and, besides, I didn't want to tell you about the scandal. It all seemed too complicated to be sorted out.'

'But you changed your mind?' he said. 'You decided to tell me?'

'Yes. The other night when I'd completed my last article it came at me, like a bolt from the blue, that I had to tell you the truth and hang the consequences. It was the only way to secure peace of mind. It was suddenly terribly important to know if you would believe me. . .'

'You love me that much?'

'I'm afraid so.'

He drew her against him and held her tightly for a long emotional moment. Then he said, 'You know I love you, Lara? You don't doubt it now, do you?'

'I don't think you would have come here tonight otherwise,' she said. 'If what you learned about me had affected you the way it affected others who didn't really care about me you would have sent my copy back by courier. You would have assumed that my not telling you myself meant that I must have been guilty.'

Lucas stroked her hair tenderly. 'I never for a moment doubted you. You see, I *know* you. I know you have more integrity than to pass off someone else's work as your own. I never doubted for an instant that you were totally innocent. But I know you well enough to guess you probably did *feel* guilty, even though you had no reason to. I understand that, Lara, because I've been through something similar myself.'

'You?' Lara was astounded.

An expression of intense pain entered his eyes. 'Three years ago a child died and it might have been my fault.'

'Oh, no!' Lara jerked up and looked at him in alarm. 'Lucas. . .'

'Some time I'll tell you the details. There was no blame attached to me except what I laid on myself, but there was a good deal of publicity. Highly emotional stuff. And my integrity was on the line. Like you, I wanted to quit and do something else, but a wise old consultant I confessed to gave me a better perspective. He said that it was one of the hazards of our profession that we expect too much of ourselves, partly because the public expect so much of us. He said that conscientious people sometimes suffered unnecessarily because of the high standards they set for themselves. He said every human was fallible and doctors, like other people, had to learn to live with it. They also had to learn to live with misunderstanding and misinterpretation, and sometimes being misjudged. So I did. But now and then I'm reminded. Like what happened to you, it's a ghost that occasionally haunts and will never go away completely.'

'I've seen you look sombre sometimes,' Lara said. 'I felt there was something deep-seated that saddened you, and also made you angry.'

'Angry with myself,' he said.

'Was that why you didn't want a Press observer in your theatres?'

'Partly. I had learned not to trust the Press.'

'But you trusted me?'

He chuckled. 'Not at first. It was simply that I just couldn't bear to let you out of my sight when I'd only just met you again.' He looked at her for a moment, then said in a new lighter tone, 'I think we've had enough of confessions, enough soul-searching for one night. Why don't you heat up the coffee, and then. . .?' He paused, smiling.

'And then?' Lara prompted.

His dark eyes had a teasing glint. 'We could go out dancing, to a nightclub, a late show. . .or. . .'

'Or what?'

'We could stay home and talk about getting married. I'm going to insist on setting a very tight deadline!'

Lara kissed him. 'I don't think I'm in the mood for nightclubs, or late shows or dancing.'

'What are you in the mood for?' Lucas asked, nibbling her lips.

'You,' she whispered. 'Just you, darling.'

'Well, since I happen to be in the mood for you, my sweet and lovely Lara, there seems to be no problem,' Lucas said softly as he deepened the kiss.

4 MEDICAL ROMANCES
AND 2 FREE GIFTS
From Mills & Boon

Capture all the excitement, intrigue and emotion of the busy medical world by accepting four FREE Medical Romances, plus a FREE cuddly teddy and special mystery gift. Then if you choose, go on to enjoy 4 more exciting Medical Romances every month! Send the coupon below at once to:

**MILLS & BOON READER SERVICE, FREEPOST
PO BOX 236, CROYDON, SURREY CR9 9EL.**
No stamp required

✂ --- ➤

YES! Please rush me my 4 Free Medical Romances and 2 Free Gifts! Please also reserve me a Reader Service Subscription. If I decide to subscribe, I can look forward to receiving 4 Medical Romances every month for just £5.80 delivered direct to my door. Post and packing is free, and there's a free Mills & Boon Newsletter. If I choose not to subscribe I shall write to you within 10 days – I can keep the books and gifts whatever I decide. I can cancel or suspend my subscription at any time. I am over 18.

EP02D

Name (Mr/Mrs/Ms) _____

Address _____

_____

_____ Postcode _____

Signature _____

— MEDICAL ♥ ROMANCE —

The books for your enjoyment this month are:

MEDICAL DECISIONS Lisa Cooper
DEADLINE LOVE Judith Worthy
NO TIME FOR ROMANCE Kathleen Farrell
RELATIVE ETHICS Caroline Anderson

♥   ♥   ♥   ♥   ♥

Treats in store!

Watch next month for the following absorbing stories:

ALL FOR LOVE Margaret Barker ·
HOMETOWN HOSPITAL Lydia Balmain
LOVE CHANGES EVERYTHING Laura MacDonald
A QUESTION OF HONOUR Margaret O'Neill